CW01657617

1+/A2

Welcome
anglais

5e

WORKBOOK 1

Ouvrage coordonné par
Evelyne LEDRU-GERMAIN

First name: [redacted] ....

Surname: [redacted] ....

Year: [redacted]

School address: ....

....

Evelyne LEDRU-GERMAIN
Collège Hippolyte-Rémy, Coulommiers
Lycée Jules-Ferry, Coulommiers

Nathalie HOLLINKA-ROUSSELLE
Collège Beau-Soleil, Chelles

Avec la collaboration de
Sandy LOCKHART
Formatrice au Greta Tertiaire Nord 77

Hatier

Sommaire

Édition : Aurélie Andrey, Samuel Briand-Favard • **Relecture** : Élise Bradbury, Kirill Ivanitski • **Maquette** : Studio Favre & Lhaïk, Natacha Marmouget • **Mise en page** : Natacha Marmouget • **Illustrations** : Sylvain Frécon (pp. 18, 19, 25, 31, 43, 46, 51, 53, 58, 63, 75), Illustratek (p. 80, 81, 84), Mauro Mazzari (pp. 7, 8, 9, 10, 11, 14, 15, 16, 17, 18, 20, 21, 31, 32, 34, 50, 93), Benoît Springer (pp. 3, 9, 10, 15, 32, 33, 37, 39, 49, 51, 55, 69, 70, 75, 77, 81) • **Iconographie** : Valérie Massignon / XYZèbre, Hatier Illustrations • ***Spotlights*** : © Hatier 2012. Avec Francesca Gray, Jameel Sardharwalla, Kyle Stanger et Victoria Ubochi • **Cartographie** : Edigraphie • **Photogravure** : APEX, La Turquoise

Crédits photographiques : p. 10 : ph © Steve Vidler / Alamy ; **p. 24-a** : ph © Photolibrary / Getty Images ; **p. 24-b** : ph © Photolibrary / Getty Images ; **p. 24-c** : ph © Ron Chapple / Corbis ; **p. 24-d** : ph © Collection Dagli Orti / Museum of the City of New York ; **p. 40-1** : ph © Hanoteau / Archives Hatier ; **p. 40-2** : ph © on Miller / Novapix ; **p. 40-3** : ph © Natural History Museum of London / Biosphoto ; **p. 40-4** : ph © Dorling Kindersley / Getty Images ; **p. 40-5** : ph © Pascal Goetgheluck / Biosphoto ; **p. 45-a** : ph © Photolibrary / Getty Images ; **p. 45-b** : ph © Photolibrary / Getty Images ; **p. 63-a** : ph © La ruée vers l'or - Charlie Chaplin - Roy Export SAS ; **p. 63-b** : ph © Photo12 et © Roy Export SAS ; **p. 63-c** : ph © Jörg Hackemann / FOTOLIA ; **p. 69-a** : ph © Rudy K / Alamy ; **p. 69-b** : ph © Axel Leschinski / Alamy ; **p. 85** : avec l'aimable autorisation de la Mairie de Bayeux ; **p. 87** : ph © NMM, Greenwich / Leemanse ; **p. 92-a et b** : THE GOLD RUSH (LA RUÉE VERS L'OR) de Charles Chaplin. Copyright © 1942 Roy Export S.A.S. All Rights Reserved. Renewed: Copyright © 1969 Roy Export S.A.S. All Rights Reserved.

Crédits texte : p. 38 : (WHAT A) WONDERFUL WORLD, Words and Music by SAM COOKE, HERB ALPERT and LOU ADLER, Copyright © 1959 (Renewed) ABKCO MUSIC, INC., 85 Fifth Avenue, New York, NY 10003. All Rights Reserved. Used by Permission.

© Hatier Paris 2012, ISBN 978-2-218-95501-3 4450490

Achevé d' imprimer en Italie par Rotolito Lombarda - dépôt légal n° 95501-3/04 - Juin 2015

Comprendre les consignes

Voici les consignes que tu trouveras dans ton *Workbook*.

a speech balloon: *une bulle de parole*
a caption: *une légende*
a chart: *un tableau*
a clue: *un indice*
a label: *une étiquette*
a mistake: *une erreur*
a sentence: *une phrase*

Check: *Vérifie.*

Circle:

Count:

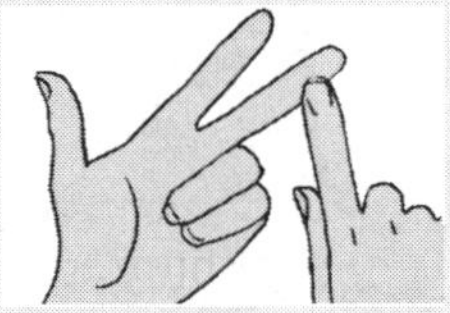

Cross the odd one out: *Barre l'intrus.*

Draw:

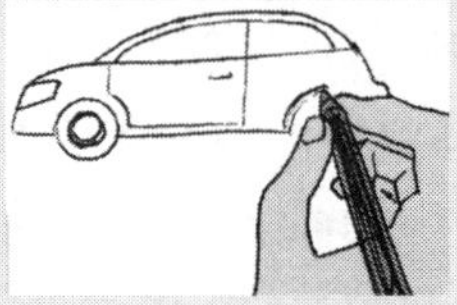

Fill in the blanks: *Complète les espaces.*

Find / Spot the differences:
Trouve / Repère les différences.

Highlight:

Match / Link:

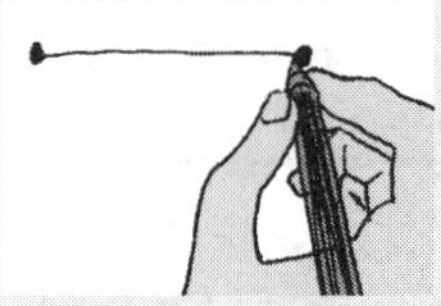

Number: *Numérote.*

Quiz your friends:
Interroge tes camarades.

Report: *Fais un compte rendu.*

Tick:

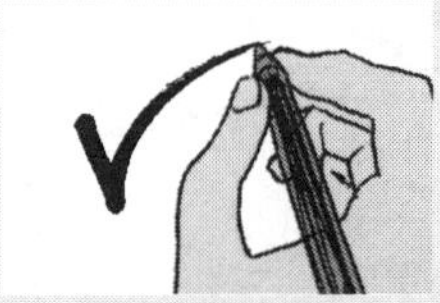

Underline:

The sound bags

Tu as appris à reconnaître plusieurs symboles phonétiques.
Regroupe les mots contenant le même son.

PART 2

➪ Manuel, *p. 19*

1 • Complète l'étiquette du sac 1 avec le symbole du son-voyelle de *butter*.
Complète l'étiquette du sac 2 avec le symbole du son-voyelle de *bread*.
Aide-toi de la boîte *Words* de ton manuel, p. 19.

2 • Classe les mots de la liste suivante dans le sac qui leur correspond.
double • bed • hungry • breakfast • yuck • red • love

1

2

PART 3

➪ Manuel, *p. 21*

1 • Complète les étiquettes des sacs 3, 4 et 5 avec les symboles des diphtongues (sons composés de deux sons-voyelles) de *lake, ghost* et *mile*.
Aide-toi de la boîte *Words* de ton manuel, p. 21.

2 • Classe les mots de la liste suivante dans le sac qui leur correspond.
no • eight • fine • name • know • late • slow • chain • hotel • right • sign • go • like

3

4

5

PART 4

⇨ Manuel, *p. 23*

1 • Complète les étiquettes des sacs 6 et 7 avec les symboles des voyelles longues de *turn* et *between*.
Aide-toi de la boîte *Words* de ton manuel, p. 23.

2 • Classe les mots de la liste suivante dans le sac qui leur correspond.
girl • sheep • first • tea • beans • surname • thirsty

Astuce

Les deux points (:) indiquent que la voyelle est longue.
Ils ressemblent à un sablier... alors prends ton temps pour prononcer ces voyelles !

6

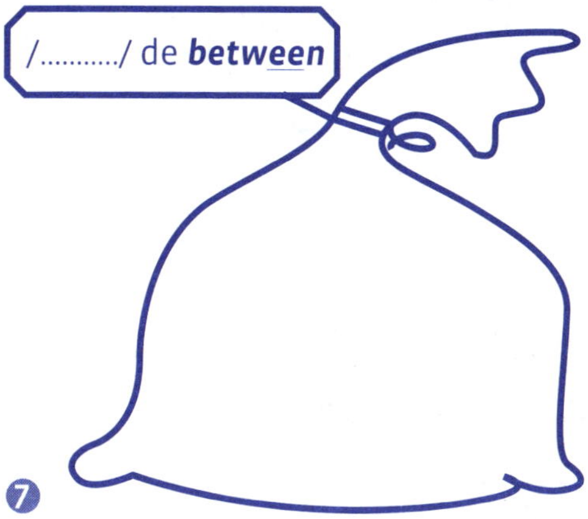

7

PART 5

⇨ Manuel, *p. 24*

1 • Complète les étiquettes des sacs 8 et 9 avec les symboles des sons-voyelles de *actor* et *ball*.
Aide-toi de la boîte *Words* de ton manuel, p. 24.

2 • Classe les mots de la liste suivante dans le sac qui leur correspond.
have • black • that • born • back • talk • map

Astuce

Lorsque tu rencontres un nouveau son dans une leçon, crée un nouveau ***sound bag***.

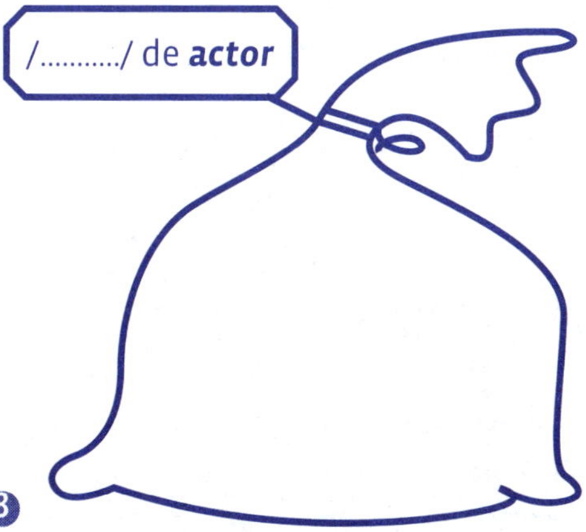

8

9

A trip to Scotland

PART 1

Arrival in Scotland

Play with your alphabet. ➪ Manuel, *p. 16*

Utilise l'alphabet anglais pour comprendre ces messages.
Ex. : U2 ➔ You too!

ICU! ➔ .... RUOK? ➔ ....
B4U ➔ .... 2EZ! ➔ ....

A. At the airport ➪ Manuel, *p. 16*

1 • Tick the correct answer.
It is ☒ in the morning ❑ in the afternoon ❑ in the evening.

2 • Circle the correct answers.
Mr McLee's parents are
(Scottish) English American.
They're from
Chicago London (Edinburgh.)

3 • The McLee family: write their first names and the children's ages.
The father: ....Brian.... McLee
The mother: ....Helen.... McLee
The boy: ....Dylan.... McLee (age: ..13..)
The girl: ....Ema.... McLee (age: ..11..)

4 • Recap.
The McLees are ....American....
They live in ....Chicago...., but Mr McLee's family is from ....Edinburgh.... .

TOOLS ➪ Manuel, *p. 17*

Se présenter.

• **Donne un âge avec le verbe *be*.**
*I'**m** eleven and a half, I'**m** not twelve.*
*You'**re** twelve, you **are**n't thirteen.*

• **Donne une origine avec le verbe *be*.**
*He **is from** Scotland.*
(Pour un garçon ou un homme.)
*She **isn't from** Edinburgh.*
(Pour une fille ou une femme.)

• **Donne une nationalité avec le verbe *be*.**
*We **are** English.*
*They **are** American.*

• **Dis où tu habites.**
*I **live** in Scotland. I live at 25 Campbell Avenue, in Edinburgh.*

Se renseigner sur une personne.

• **Renseigne-toi sur une nationalité.**
*"**What**'s your nationality?"*

• **Renseigne-toi sur un âge.**
*"**How old** are you?"*

• **Renseigne-toi sur une ville ou un pays d'origine.**
*"**Where** are you **from**?"*

RAOUL

B. Arrival at the hotel

➪ Manuel, *p. 17*

1 • What number is the McLees' room?

❑ 16 ❑ 60 ☒ 15 ❑ 50

2 • Complete the information about the McLees' bags and suitcases.

I can't see my bag is green.

I can't see you bag is pink.

Where is you suitcase is grey.

it's black, not suitcase is brown.

3 • Recap: Fill in the names and the labels.

Fergus has got the Suitcase trolley and not the bag on trolley.

The Dylan trolley The Emma trolley

TOOLS

➪ Manuel, *p. 17*

Parler de la possession.

• Parle de ce que tu possèdes avec les déterminants possessifs.

*It's **my** suitcase.*

*It's **your** suitcase.*

*It's **her** suitcase.* *It's **his** suitcase.*

*It's **our** suitcase.*

➪ Manuel, *ex.2, p. 168*

*It's **their** suitcase.*

Attention : Pour choisir le déterminant, regarde bien **à qui** appartient l'objet et accorde le déterminant avec le possesseur !

• Renseigne-toi sur le propriétaire d'un objet.

***Whose** book is it?*

Utilise ***whose*** suivi d'un nom.

Si ce nom est au **pluriel**, pense à **accorder** le sujet et le verbe !

➪ Manuel, *ex.4a, p. 168*

*Whose **shoes** are **they**?*

• Indique le propriétaire d'un objet ou un lien de parenté.

Donne le nom du propriétaire suivi de **'s**.

*It is Jenny**'s** bag.*

*He is Jenny**'s** brother.*

Pense à accorder le verbe.

They are Bob's shoes.

Attention avec un propriétaire pluriel, on ne met que l'apostrophe.

It's the McLees' room.

Do you remember?

1 • Complète les phrases avec le verbe *be*.

a. I am French.

b. It ...... my passport.

c. You are from Lyon.

d. We are from the USA.

e. She is twelve.

f. They are Scottish.

g. He is American.

2 • Remplace les sujets soulignés par un pronom personnel.

a. Mr McLee is American.
he

b. Mrs McLee is from Chicago.
she

c. Emma and Dylan are American.
they

d. My sister and I are from Scotland.
you

e. My passport is British.
It

f. The passports are in my bag.
thay

3 • Retrouve les questions qui ont été posées.

a. "What's his name ?" "His name's Matt."
b. "How old is she ?" "She's twelve and a half."
c. "Where do you live from ?" "They're Scottish."
d. "Where are you from ?" "He's from Glasgow."

4 • Observe le dessin puis présente Ashley Macfire.

Astuce

Pense à vérifier que tu as utilisé le bon pronom personnel et la bonne forme du verbe *be* !

Ashley is 12 years old, she from London
she hese gote a litle browers and she lives
25 standars Road London

5 • Regarde les objets suivants et indique à qui ils appartiennent.

a.

It's got BoB.

b.

It is got Mr and Mrs Mclee

c.

They are got Emma

6 • Exprime les liens de parenté puis note le déterminant possessif entre parenthèses.

a. Emma / Dylan

Emma is small Dylan (1 sister).

Dylan is tall Emma (1 brother).

b. Mrs McLee / Emma and Dylan

Mrs McLee is parent (1 mother).

Emma and Dylan are parent (2 children).

7 • Tu as trouvé un passeport, deux cahiers et un sac. Pose des questions pour retrouver leurs propriétaires.

How is they books

How is the passeport,

PART 2

At the hotel

A. The bedroom

➩ Manuel, *p. 18*

1 • Where are the McLees? ☐ At the reception desk. ☐ In room 15. ☐ In room 50.

2 • Listen and tick what there is in the McLees' room.

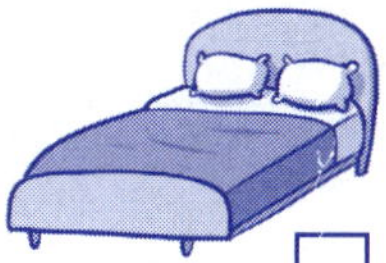 ☐

....

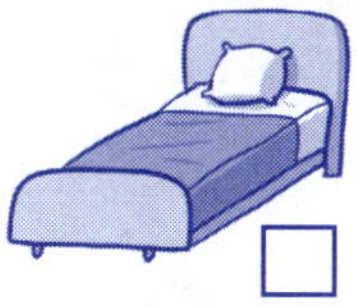 ☐

....

 ☐

....

 ☐

....

 ☐

....

 ☐

....

 ☐

....

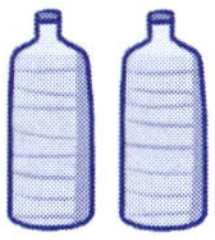 ☐

....

3 • What do Emma, Dylan and Mr McLee want? Write their names under the pictures above.

4 • Mr McLee and Dylan want to go:

☐ to the reception desk ☐ to the restaurant

☐ to bed.

5 • Recap: tick the correct answers.

a. Emma isn't happy because there isn't ☐ a mini bar
☐ an Internet connection ☐ a television.

b. Dylan isn't happy because there isn't
☐ a television ☐ an adaptor ☐ a bath.

c. Mr McLee isn't happy because there aren't any
☐ bottles of water ☐ single beds ☐ chairs.

TOOLS ➩ Manuel, *p. 19*

Se renseigner sur ce qu'il y a.

• **Pour parler de l'existence de quelque chose, utilise *there is* ou *there are*.**

***There is** a shower.*

Accorde le verbe avec le nom qui le suit.

***There are** plugs.*

• **Pour parler de ce qu'il n'y a pas, conjugue *be* à la forme négative.**

***There isn't** a television.*

***There aren't** any US plugs.*

Astuce

Les prises aux États-Unis et en Angleterre ne sont pas les mêmes. Les McLee doivent donc utiliser un adaptateur, qui se dit, en anglais, *an* ....

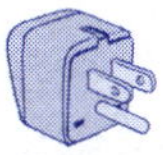

an American plug

a British plug

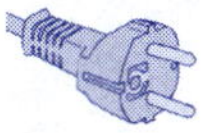

a French plug

Astuce

Le petit déjeuner britannique est plus consistant que le nôtre ! C'est presque un repas ! On y trouve souvent des *baked beans* !

B. Breakfast time

➪ Manuel, *p. 19*

1 • Fill in the labels.

croissants • bread • butter • jam • fruit juice • tea • cereal • bacon • eggs • sausage • tomato • mushrooms

2 • Draw the appropriate symbols:

♥ ♥, ♥, ~~♥ ♥~~, ~~♥~~.

Dylan : ....  .... 

.... haggis

Emma: .... 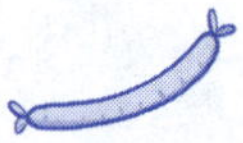 .... 

....  .... haggis

3 • Recap.

Dylan .... mushrooms

and Emma .... sausages.

She .... the American breakfast.

Dylan .... his Scottish breakfast

but Emma .... it!

TOOLS

➪ Manuel, *p. 19*

Parler de ses goûts.

➪ Manuel, *ex.9, p. 169*

***Do** you **like** haggis?*

*I **love** haggis.* *I **like** haggis.*

♥ ♥ ♥

*I **don't like** haggis* *I **hate** haggis*

~~♥~~ ~~♥♥~~

***Does** he **like** haggis?*

*He **loves** haggis. He **doesn't like** haggis.*

Utiliser les déterminants.

• Pour parler de quelque chose <u>en général</u>, ne mets pas d'article.

I like Ø mushrooms.

• Pour parler de quelque chose de précis, utilise l'article *the*.

*I like **the** mushrooms in this breakfast.*

• Pour parler d'un élément <u>quelconque</u>, utilise l'article *a* ou *an* devant un son-voyelle.

*There's **a** mushroom and **an** apple on the table.*

➪ Manuel, *ex.3, p. 168*

Do you remember?

1 • Regarde le dessin ci-dessous et explique ce qu'il y a au petit déjeuner.

....

....

2 • Regarde le dessin ci-dessous et explique ce qu'il y a dans cette chambre.

....

....

....

3 • Regarde le dessin ci-dessous et parle des goûts de Sara.

Sara ....

....

....

4 • Parle de tes goûts pour des aliments représentés ci-dessus.

....

....

5 • Construis des questions à l'aide des éléments proposés.

you / like / pancakes / ? ➔ ....

your brother / like / tea / ? ➔ ....

6 • Complète les phrases suivantes avec *the*, a / *an* ou Ø.

a. I love .... cereal.

b. Do you like .... bacon?

c. Look, there's .... orange and .... banana on the table.

d. I love .... pancakes your mother makes!

7 • Tu envoies un mail à ton correspondant anglais.

Ton correspondant t'a demandé des renseignements sur ce qu'il y a dans ta chambre et ce que tu aimes manger au petit déjeuner. Donne-lui les informations attendues et pose-lui quelques questions en retour.

Astuces

- Pense à **inverser *there*** et ***be*** dans les questions et à **accorder** le verbe.
- Relie tes phrases avec ***and*** et ***but***.
- Pense à **varier** les verbes de goût !

Hi ....,

How are you?

So, in my bedrooom, ...

....

What about your bedroom? ....

....

Concerning breakfast, ...

....

What about you? ....

See you! xx

PART 3

Tourist information

A. Visiting Scotland

Manuel, p. 20

1 • Listen and circle the attractions they suggest.

a. Mr McLee suggests lakes castles gardens.

b. Mrs McKenzie suggests lochs castles gardens.

2 • Complete the sentences or tick the correct answers.

a. Their suggestions are ❑ different ❑ not different.

b. Dylan is interested in .... Ness.

c. Distance from the hotel: ❑ 5 miles ❑ 55 miles ❑ 155 miles.

3 • Tick the correct answers.

a. How many lakes are there near the hotel? ❑ 7. ❑ 10. ❑ 11.

b. The bagpipers are ❑ in the hotel ❑ in the street.

c. How many bagpipers are there?

❑ 2 or 3. ❑ 5 or 6. ❑ 10 or 12.

d. Dylan ❑ likes ❑ doesn't like this music.

4 • Recap.

.... is far from the hotel, but there are lots of .... near the hotel.

Dylan .... the bagpipes because they are loud.

Mr and Mrs McLee .... Dylan's music because it's loud.

> **TOOLS** ➪ Manuel, *p. 21*
>
> **Se renseigner sur un lieu.**
>
> • **Renseigne-toi sur un lieu.**
> ***Where** is the castle?*
>
> • **Renseigne-toi sur une quantité.**
> ***How many** lakes are there?*
>
> **Attention !** ***How many*** est toujours suivi d'un nom au pluriel. Pense à accorder le verbe.

B. An interesting attraction

➪ Manuel, *p. 21*

1 • Listen and number the attractions in the correct order.

☐ Borthwick Castle ☐ The Writers' Museum ☐ Rosslyn Chapel

☐ Royal Botanic Garden

2 • Listen again and spot the problems.

Attraction 1 ●	● is the house of a woman ghost.
Attraction 2 ●	● is ❑ boring ❑ interesting for Dylan.
Attraction 3 ●	● ❑ opens ❑ doesn't open on Sundays.
Attraction 4 ●	● is very expensive.

3 • Fill in the information.

Rosslyn Chapel

Rosslyn Chapel

Opens from .... to ....

Adults £............... (≈ $................)

Children £..........

> **TOOLS** ➪ Manuel, *p. 21*
>
> **Dire l'heure.**
>
> *It's **ten** past one.* — ten: minutes, one: heure
> *It's **twenty** to six.* — twenty: minutes, six: heure
>
> Indique d'abord les **minutes**. Puis choisis ***past*** si l'aiguille des minutes est à droite, ***to*** si elle est à gauche. Termine par les heures. Utilise ***quarter*** pour dire « quart » et ***half*** pour dire « demi ».
>
> **Se renseigner sur un prix.** ➪ Manuel, *ex.4b, p. 168*
>
> • **Pour demander un prix.**
> ***How much** is it? **How much** are they?*
>
> • **Pour donner un prix.**
> *It's five **pounds** fifty **(£5.50)**.*
> *It's ten **dollars** **($10)**.*
>
> **Attention !** Le symbole de la livre sterling anglaise **(£)** et **le symbole du dollar américain ($) s'écrivent avant** les nombres mais **se disent après** le premier nombre.

4 • Recap.

Emma ❑ thinks ❑ doesn't think there is a .... in Borthwick Castle.

Dylan is ❑ interested ❑ not interested ❑ afraid.

Do you remember?

1 • Renseigne-toi pour savoir combien de musées il y a à *Edinburgh*.

....

2 • Retrouve les questions qui ont été posées sur le château.

a. ....
....? — *25 rooms.*

b. ....
....? — *At 9 am.*

c. ....? — *It's in Edinburgh, 10 miles from the hotel.*

d. ....? — *It's £2.10.*

3 • Note l'heure en toutes lettres.

a 
b 
c 
d 

It's .... It's .... It's .... It's ....

4 • Note les prix suivants en toutes lettres.

a. £1.20 ....

b. $2 ....

c. £8.50 ....

PART 4

A mysterious castle ...

A. On the road

➪ Manuel, *p. 22*

1 • Listen and draw the McLees' route on the map. Where must they go?

2 • Tick the correct pictures.

Mrs McLee mustn't ❑ 

❑  because the sheep are ❑  ❑  now.

3 • Recap: Look at the map and complete.

The McLees .... turn left after the bridge.
Then they .... take the first road on the right.
They must drive .... on after the bridge.
Mrs McLee .... drive fast because there are a lot of .... on the road and it's raining cats and dogs!

Astuce

Quand il pleut beaucoup, les Anglais disent *It's raining cats and dogs!*
Cela ne veut pas dire que des animaux tombent du ciel!

TOOLS ➪ Manuel, *p. 23*

Parler d'obligations et d'interdictions. ➪ Manuel, *ex.23a, p. 173*

- Utilise ***must*** pour indiquer ce que quelqu'un doit faire.
  *You **must** stop!*
  BV

- Utilise ***mustn't*** pour indiquer ce qu'il ne faut pas faire.
  ***I mustn't** honk!*
  BV

Must et ***mustn't*** sont suivis de la **base verbale** à toutes les personnes !

B. A strange guide

➪ Manuel, p. 23

1 • Listen and tick the correct answers.

a. The McLees ❑ can ❑ can't visit Macstrange Castle today.

b. They ❑ can take photos ❑ mustn't take photos in the castle.

2 • Listen and tick the correct picture of the Black Tower.

❑ 

❑ 

❑ 

3 • Tick the correct answers.

a. The McLees ❑ can ❑ can't visit the Black Tower because ❑ it isn't open today ❑ it's too expensive.

b. The guide says ❑ there is ❑ there isn't a ghost in the tower.

4 • Recap.

The McLees .... the Black Tower today because it's closed, but they .... the castle!

TOOLS ➪ Manuel, p. 23

Parler de possibilités et de permissions.

• Utilise *can* pour parler de ce que tu peux faire ou non.

➪ Manuel, ex.23c, p. 173

*They **can** drive to the castle.*
BV

*We **can't** visit the Tower today.*
BV

***Can** I open the door, please?*
BV

• *Can* et *can't* sont suivis de la base verbale à toutes les personnes.

Do you remember?

1 • Complète la légende des panneaux.

a 

b 

c 

d 

e 

a. You must turn ....

b. You mustn't turn ....

c. You mustn't turn ....

d. You must go ....

e. We can .... here.

2 • Complète la légende de chaque dessin en indiquant où se trouvent les moutons.

a.  The sheep is .... the trees.

c.  The .... are ....

b.  ....

3 • Complète les phrases avec *must, mustn't, can* ou *can't.*

a. You .... slow down. There's a horse in the middle of the road!

b. .... we close the window, please? It's cold.

c. You .... honk next to a hospital.

d. My parents .... drive me to school. Our car's at the garage.

e. Superman .... fly: he's a superhero!

f. "............... I go now, please?"   "No, you ...."

PART 5

The mystery

A. An old ghost

➪ Manuel, *p. 24*

1 • Listen and tick Dylan's mood.

❑    ❑    ❑ 

2 • Tick the correct answer.

a. James is ❑ an actor ❑ a guide ❑ a ghost.

b. In the film, he is ❑ Angus Macstrange ❑ Angus's brother.

c. Angus and his brother ❑ were born ❑ weren't born in the castle.

d. Angus was born in ❑ 1537 ❑ 1547 ❑ 1567.

e. Alastair was born in ❑ 1544 ❑ 1548 ❑ 1550.

3 • Complete the drawings and the captions.

First name: ANGUS
Surname: ....
Age: ....

First name: ....
Surname: ....
Age: ....

4 • Recap: Write the dates in letters.

a. The Macstrange brothers ....
.... in the Black Tower. Angus was born
in .... and his brother
.... in ....

b. These ghosts are very strange! Angus ....
a chain but he .... a ball, but his brother
.... a chain!

TOOLS ➪ Manuel, *p. 24*

Dire des dates et nombres.

• **Dis les dates précédant** ➪**Manuel,** *ex.6a, p. 169* **l'an 2000 par tranche de deux chiffres.**
19 96 ➔ *nineteen ninety-six*
Attention ! 1903 ➔ *nineteen **o** three*

• **Entre l'an 2000 et 2009, utilise le mot** ***thousand*** **(mille).**
2007 ➔ *two thousand and seven.*

• **Après 2010, tu peux utiliser** ***thousand*** **ou dire la date par tranche de deux chiffres.**
2013 ➔ *two thousand and thirteen* ou *twenty thirteen*

• **Utilise le mot** ***hundred*** **pour dire « cent ».**
428 ➔ *four **hundred** and twenty-eight*
Remarque : on dit *and* entre le chiffre des centaines et des dizaines !

Préciser ce que l'on a ou non.

• **Utilise l'expression** ***have got*** **pour parler de ce que tu as ou non.**
***Have** you **got** a computer?*
*I've **got** a dog.*
(have)
*They **haven't got** a cat.*

• ***Have*** **devient** ***has*** **à la troisième personne du singulier.**
***Has** he **got** a car?*
*He's **got** a computer, but he **hasn't got** a car.*
(has)

B. What's wrong?

➪ Manuel, *p. 24*

1 • Highlight the mistakes in Angus's identity card.

FIRST NAME: Angus
SURNAME:
DATE OF BIRTH:
PLACE OF BIRTH:
The Tower,
Castle,
FAMILY: A

2 • Correct the mistakes.

a. ....

b. ....

c. ....

d. ....

3 • Read this text about Angus. Find the two mistakes and correct them.

> Visitors to Macstrange Castle can visit the Black Tower, where Angus and Alastair the famous Irish ghosts live. The legend says Angus hasn't got a ball or a chain. Come and visit the castle when you're in Scotland and don't forget to say hello to the Macstrange brothers!

a. ....

b. ....

DID YOU KNOW?

Regarde l'illustration en haut de la carte page II au début de ton manuel et coche la bonne réponse.
C'est une fleur de : ❑ chardon ❑ pissenlit ❑ coquelicot.
La fleur de .... (en anglais « *thistle* ») est le symbole de l'Écosse !
L'Angleterre (*England*), le Pays de Galles (*Wales*) et l'Irlande (*Ireland*) ont également des symboles nationaux.
Regarde à nouveau la carte et complète le tableau ci-contre.

Country	Symbol
Scotland	 t............................
....	 rose
....	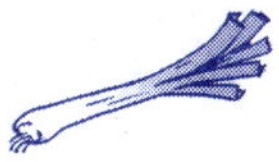 leek
....	 shamrock

Do you remember?

1 • Réponds à cette question te concernant. Écris la date en lettres.

"When were you born?" "I ....

CLASSE CD • 1 13

2 • Écoute les nombres et écris-les en chiffres.

a. .... b. .... c. .... d. .... e. .... f. .... g. .... h. ....

3 • Écris les dates ci-dessous en lettres.

a. 1668 ➔ ....

b. 1873 ➔ ....

c. 1440 ➔ ....

d. 2012 ➔ ....

4 • Écris les nombres ci-dessous en lettres.

a. 623 ➔ ....

b. 550 ➔ ....

c. 912 ➔ ....

d. 111 ➔ ....

5 • Remets les mots dans l'ordre pour former des phrases correctes.
Attention, il y a un intrus dans chaque phrase.

a. got / teacher / my / has / have / a / dog / .

....

b. new / got / you / has / trainers / have / ?

....

c. our / books / English / we / got / haven't / hasn't / .

....

d. has / brother / car / a / your / got / have / ?

....

6 • Regarde ce que Tim et Tina ont emporté dans leurs sacs à dos.
Regarde leur bulle de pensée et déduis-en ce qu'ils n'ont ni l'un, ni l'autre!

Astuce

Utilise ***and*** et ***but*** pour relier tes phrases.

....

....

CULTURE CORNER

Scotland's many faces

Manuel, *pp. 26-27*

A Discover Scottish traditions

Complete the crossword.

Across

1. A musical instrument.
3. A monster's name.
4. People from Scotland.

Down

2. A coloured design on a kilt.
5. A city in the Highlands.

B Words!

CLASSE CD 1 14

a. Listen to these Scottish words and give the correct number

.... wee (small)

.... Sassenach (English person)

.... bairn (child)

.... gairden (garden)

.... auld (old)

.... aye (yes)

CLASSE CD 1 15

b. Listen to the sentence in Scottish. Then write it in English!

....

C Scottish humour

Write funny balloons.

....
....
....
....

....
....
....
....

At Mrs Cooper's

⇨ Manuel, p. 28

Do you remember the video?

Write captions or fill in the balloons.

In London ...

PART 1

1

2

....

....

3

....

....

PART 2

4

....

5

....

....

6

PROJECT A funny place ➪ Manuel, p. 29

Imagine and present a funny hotel in Scotland.

Fill in this chart about your hotel. Don't forget one or two strange things or surprises.

.... HOTEL

INFORMATION

Hotel facilities:

❑ TV ❑ Internet connection ❑ restaurant

❑ bathroom ❑ double bed ❑ single bed

Car park: ❑ Yes. ❑ No.

Swimming pool: ❑ Yes. ❑ No.

Things to see near the hotel:

....

....

....

....

....

....

Price: £........ per night

Restaurant opening hours:

Breakfast from .... to ....

Lunch from .... to ....

Dinner from .... to ....

Hotel rules:

You must ....

....

You mustn't ....

....

WORKSHOP 1

From the UK to the USA

Listen

➪ Manuel, p. 31

1 • Listen to Justin and write the correct caption under the photographs.

The White House • The Washington Monument • Largo

....
....

2 • Listen to Justin and tick the correct answers.

a. The Browns are ❑ British ❑ American.

b. Justin ❑ is an only child ❑ has got a brother.

c. ❑ Mr Brown ❑ Mrs Brown is a great cook.

d. The Browns are in the USA for ❑ the holiday ❑ a long time.

DID YOU KNOW?

Washington, D.C. (District of Columbia) is the capital city of the United States of America. That's why the president lives there, in the White House. The first president, George Washington, gave it his name in 1791.

George Washington
(1732 – 1799)

TAKE 1 I hate housework!

Warm up. ➪ Manuel, p. 32

Write the correct expression under the pictures.

hoover • set the table • clear the table • feed the cat • dust • load the dishwasher • take out the rubbish

a 

....

b 

....

c 

....

d 

....

e 

....

f 

....

g 

....

A Life at the Browns' ➪ Manuel, p. 32

1 • Listen and tick the correct answer.

It's ❑ the morning ❑ the afternoon ❑ the evening.

2 • Listen and circle the chores they're talking about.

set the table	....	feed the cat	....
do the cooking	....	dust	....
clear the table	....	tidy the rooms	....
wash the floor	....	take out the rubbish	....
make his / her bed	....	hoover	....
load the dishwasher	....	do the shopping	....

3 • Who is supposed to do these chores?

Write the names (Alex, Justin, Lily, Mr Brown, Mrs Brown, all the family or ?) next to the chores in **2.**

4 • Cross out the chores Justin often or always forgets.

5 • Circle the correct answers.

a. Mrs Brown thinks Justin is helpful lazy hard-working absent-minded.

b. Alex thinks his brother is helpful lazy hard-working absent-minded.

6 • Recap.

Everybody .... with the housework.

Justin is ❑ happy ❑ not happy ❑ sorry because he thinks his brother and his sister ❑ help a lot at home ❑ don't help a lot at home.

Conclude.

I think Justin is ❑ lazy ❑ helpful.

Grammar bag **Le présent simple (1) : les formes affirmative et négative**

Get it.

■ La forme affirmative

1. Observe les phrases suivantes. Encadre le verbe en rouge et souligne le sujet en bleu.

He sets the table every day. *I often help at home.*

2. Dans ces phrases, il est question ❑ d'actions habituelles ❑ d'actions en cours ❑ d'actions terminées.

● Pour conjuguer un verbe au présent simple, on ajoute un .... à la .... personne du .... à la **forme affirmative**.

Attention !

Lorsque le verbe se termine par *-ch, -sh, -o, -s, -x* ou *-z*, on ajoute .... à la 3e personne du singulier.

Ex. : *He watch..... TV.*

Lorsque le verbe se termine par *-y*, celui-ci se transforme en .... avant la terminaison.

Ex. : *He never tid........ his room!*

■ La forme négative

1. Observe les phrases suivantes.

He doesn't help at home! *I don't make my bed in the morning.*

2. Encadre le verbe en rouge et souligne l'auxiliaire en noir.

● Pour conjuguer un verbe au présent simple à la **forme négative**, on ajoute ....
(ou .... à la 3e personne du singulier) devant la ....

Attention !
Pour parler d'habitudes, on utilise :

– des **adverbes de fréquence** (*never, sometimes, often, always ...*) qui se placent ....
le verbe d'action. Ex. : *He* ***often*** *plays tennis.*

Mais les adverbes de fréquence se placent .... le verbe *be.* Ex. : *He's* ***often*** *late!*

– des **expressions de fréquence** (comme *every* ....) qui se placent en fin de phrase.
Ex. : *He makes his bed* ***every day****.*

In the bag.

1 Mets les phrases suivantes à la 3e personne du singulier.

a. I make my bed every day. → ....
b. They don't often help. → He ....
c. We wash the car at the weekend. → Dad ....
d. They never tidy their rooms. → My sister ....

2 Mets les phrases suivantes à la forme négative.

a. I clean the house on Sundays. → I ....
b. She hoovers every day. → She ....

3 Construis des phrases à l'aide des éléments donnés et barre l'intrus.

a. Dad / the / dishwasher / always / loads / load. ....
....
b. I / often / he / bed / my / make. ....

The Music of English

La terminaison -s du présent simple. ➪ Manuel, *p. 32*

CLASSE CD • 1 20

a. Écoute et entoure la prononciation de la terminaison.

1. /s/ /z/ /ɪz/ comme dans *sets, makes, helps.*
2. /s/ /z/ /ɪz/ comme dans *washes, watches.*
3. /s/ /z/ /ɪz/ comme dans *plays, clears, loads.*

Rappel
Ce -s se prononce :
- /s/ après les sons /k/, /p/, /t/ ;
- /ɪz/ après les sons /s/, /ʃ/ et /z/ ;
- /z/ dans les autres cas.

b. **Complète le tableau ci-dessous en écrivant un verbe à la 3e personne dans chaque case. Puis, joue avec ton camarade.**

	A	B	C
1	....	....	....
2	....	....	....
3	....	....	....

Annoncez chacun votre tour une case et le verbe correspondant. Ex. : *A2 works.*

Si dans cette case, les terminaisons de vos verbes ont la même prononciation, dites **« *Match!* »** et coloriez la case puisque vous avez obtenu une paire !

Si leur prononciation est différente, dites **« *No match!* »** et ne coloriez pas la case puisque vous n'avez pas obtenu de paire.

How many pairs have you got in common ? ....

B A chore board

➪ Manuel, *p. 32*

1 • Listen and tick the correct answer.

a. Who is Meg? ❑ Justin's mother. ❑ Justin's sister. ❑ Justin's friend.

b. She lives ❑ in the States ❑ in England ❑ in France.

c. Justin is ❑ in a bad mood ❑ happy ❑ tired on the phone.

2 • Fill in the Browns' choreboard (A = Alex ; J = Justin ; L = Lily) and correct the mistakes.

3 • Circle the initial when someone doesn't do a chore.

4 • Recap.

Alex ❏ rarely ❏ often ❏ always does his chores.
Lily ❏ has got ❏ hasn't got a lot of chores but she ❏ always does all her chores ❏ never does her chores.
Justin ❏ always does his chores ❏ doesn't do all his chores.

Conclude.

Justin ❏ is ❏ isn't lazy but .... is lazy too. She hasn't got a lot of .... but she doesn't do them! Justin says he always .... the table but in fact, he often ....!

Grammar bag **Le présent simple (1) : la forme interrogative**

Get it.

1. Observe les phrases suivantes.

Do you often set the table? *Does he always make his bed?*

2. Encadre le verbe en rouge, souligne le sujet en bleu et l'auxiliaire en noir.

● Pour poser une question, j'utilise :
l'**auxiliaire** .... (ou .... à la 3e pers. du sing.) + le **sujet** + le **verbe** à la ....

Rappel
Dans une question, les adverbes de fréquence (*always, often*...) se placent juste **avant** la ....

Cas particulier
How often est une expression figée qui sert à se renseigner sur la fréquence.
Ex.: *How* .... *do you make your bed?*

In the bag.

Construis les questions à l'aide des mots proposés et ajoute l'élément manquant.

a. how often / he / set the table?

....

b. you / always / help your parents?

....

c. how often / they / hoover their rooms?

....

d. she / sometimes / cook?

....

Take your pen.

Your cousin is coming to stay at your house for one week. Write a note to tell him / her about the chores.

Here is how the chores are organized at home: you can help us if you want! I always set the table on ....

....

....

....

....

You're the actor!

➪ Manuel, p. 33

Fill in your ideal chore board.
Remember, everybody must help!

Astuce
Lorsque tu fais ton compte rendu, pense à utiliser des mots de liaison comme *and* et *but*.

Chores	Your family		Your partner's family	
	Who?	How often? / When?	Who?	How often? / When?
Hoover the rooms	....	....	....	....
Load the dishwasher	....	....	....	....
Set the table	....	....	....	....
Clear the table	....	....	....	....
Other chores: –	....	....	....	....
–	....	....	....	....

Do you remember?

1 • Complète le vocabulaire des corvées suivantes.

a. .... / .... the table

b. .... the dishwasher

c. .... the carpet

d. .... your bed

e. .... your room

f. .... the cat

2 • Indique la fréquence suggérée.

a 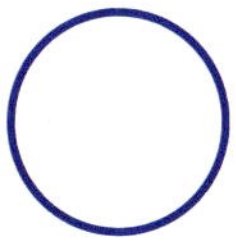

....

b 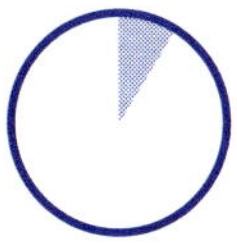

....

c 

....

d 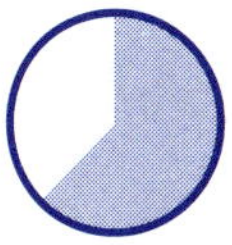

....

e 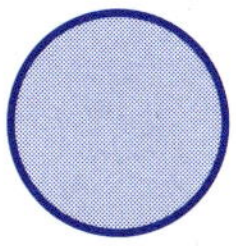

....

f 

....

g 

....

h 

....

3 • Remets les mots dans l'ordre pour former des phrases correctes.

a. washes / she / never / the / floors / .

....

b. often / you / load / do / dishwasher / how / the / ?

....

c. your / does / the / sometimes / do / brother / cooking / ?

....

d. mother / Mondays / do / my / doesn't / the shopping / on / .

....

TAKE 2 *Hobbies and activities*

Warm up.

➪ Manuel, *p. 36*

Complete with the correct verb.

a. Tommy and Prissy .... regularly.

b. Prissy can .... well because they .... a lot together.

c. They .... and .... to music together in the arena. But Prissy can't ....!

Astuce

Attention ! En français, il y a un s au mot « danse » mais en anglais, c'est un ......

He can ....!

A Who's Maggie? ➪ Manuel, p. 36

I CAN do it!

➪ Manuel, p. 35

> Comment apprendre mon vocabulaire ?

Apprends ton vocabulaire en dessinant un soleil de mots sur le thème *Hobbies and activities*.

Tu peux classer les mots par rubrique : *sporty, artistic* ...

➪ *My personality*, Manuel p. 175

1 • Listen and link the correct elements.

Mr Robinson ●	● a labrador
Maggie ●	● a PE teacher

2 • Listen and underline the days mentioned by Mr Robinson.
Circle in red the day which is a problem.

Sunday Monday Tuesday Wednesday Thursday Friday Saturday

3 • Listen and complete the missing information.

The walks are ....-hour long, so Lily can do her homework at .... o'clock.

4 • Listen and link the correct elements.

♥ ●   ♥♥ ●

● 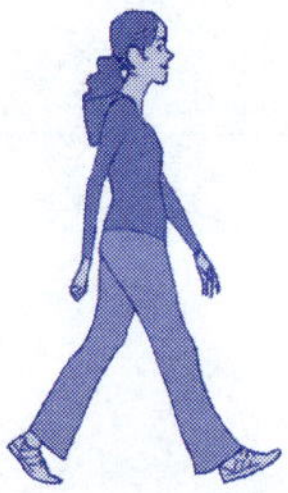

● 

● 

● 

5 • Recap: Complete the sentences.

Lily's crazy about .... and she's fond of .... and .... with them.

Conclude.

Lily's ❑ 

❑ 

because she's got a job!

Astuce

Calcule combien Lily va gagner chaque semaine.

Regarde tes réponses aux questions **2** et **3** ci-dessus, puis entoure les bonnes réponses ci-dessous.

Lily va promener Maggie	1 fois	2 fois	3 fois	par semaine.
Les promenades durent	30 minutes	1 heure	1 heure 30.	

Complète.

Lily va gagner $......... chaque semaine.

Grammar bag — L'expression des goûts

Get it.

1. Observe les phrases suivantes.

I like football.
I enjoy playing football.
He's crazy about rap music.
He's fond of listening to rap music.

2. Encadre en rouge le verbe ou l'expression de goût et souligne en noir son complément.

● Pour parler **de ce que l'on aime** faire :

on utilise **un verbe de goût** ou **une expression de goût** + { groupe .... / BV + ... }

In the bag.

Construis des phrases à l'aide des éléments donnés.

a. Tom loves / dance → ....

b. I am crazy about / animals → ....

c. They like / chocolate → ....

d. Mum is fond of / cook → ....

B Dogs!

➪ Manuel, *p. 37*

1 • Listen and link each person to their pet. Then link the pets to their names.

Mrs Miller ●	● dog ●	● Lexie
Lily ●	● cat ●	● Banjo

2 • Listen and tick the correct pictures.

a.

❑

❑

b. Banjo ♥

❑

❑

❑

3 • Recap.

Mrs Miller has got a dog, Banjo. She's really fond of ❑ him ❑ her,
and he really loves ❑ him ❑ her too!

Conclude.

Banjo ❑ is ❑ isn't a very active dog.

The Music of English

Les liaisons. ➪ Manuel, *p. 37*

En anglais, on fait des liaisons pour parler de façon plus fluide.

Généralement, quand un mot se termine par un son-consonne, et qu'il est suivi par un son-voyelle, on fait la liaison.

CLASSE CD • 1 25
a. **Écoute et note les liaisons.**

I'm fond of animals. *He's an English teacher.* *Look at it!*

Lorsqu'un mot se termine par un *–r*, ce dernier est alors prononcé afin de faire la liaison.

CLASSE CD • 1 26
b. **Écoute et repère la liaison.**

after eating

CLASSE CD • 1 27
c. **Note les liaisons dans les phrases suivantes puis écoute et vérifie.**

He loves eating an ice cream after a long walk in the park.

He's got an old armchair in his room.

Take an orange and a cup of tea.

Grammar bag — Les pronoms personnels compléments

Get it.

Observe les phrases suivantes.

Écris les pronoms personnels compléments qui conviennent :

une fille → .... un objet ou un animal inconnu → ....

un garçon → .... plusieurs objets ou plusieurs personnes → ....

In the bag.

Remplace les compléments soulignés par le pronom qui convient.

a. I'm fond of games.
....

b. They like tea.
....

c. She's crazy about Beyoncé.
....

d. I don't like your brother.
....

e. I love your friends!
....

Take your pen.

Tu cherches un correspondant anglais. Complète la fiche de renseignements et écris quelques phrases pour préciser tes goûts.

I'm fond of ...
I'm crazy about ...
I enjoy ...

Astuce

N'oublie pas de préciser également ce que tu n'aimes pas pour trouver un correspondant qui te convienne vraiment !
I don't like ... *I hate ...*

First name: ....
Surname: ....
Age: ....
Country: ....
Pets: ....
Likes and dislikes: ....
....
....
....
....

Do you remember?

1 • Écris de mémoire :

a. deux verbes associés à l'équitation.
....

b. trois verbes associés à l'eau.
....

c. deux verbes décrivant des activités artistiques.
....

d. un verbe associé à l'entraînement.
....

TAKE 2 Hobbies and activities

2 • Lis chaque phrase et écris le symbole qui convient: ♥, ♥♥, ~~♥~~, ~~♥♥~~.

a. She doesn't like diving. ....

b. They hate swimming. ....

c. Suzy's fond of reading thrillers. ....

d. He's crazy about horror films! ....

e. We enjoy walking in the park. ....

3 • Remets les mots dans l'ordre pour former des phrases correctes.

a. crazy / horses / She / is / about / riding / .

....

b. very / parents / good /singing / are / My / at / .

....

4 • Souligne le pronom personnel complément dans chaque phrase, puis remplace-le par un nom ou un groupe nominal adapté.

a. I don't like her. → ....

b. Can you see them in the trees? → ....

c. They're really fond of him. → ....

d. I hate it. → ....

TAKE 3 School clubs

Warm up. ⇨ Manuel, p. 40

Which school club are they in? Complete the sentences.

a. My brother likes playing the guitar. He's in the ....

b. We want to protect nature, so we are members of the ....

c. My cousin loves drawing clothes, so he goes to the .... on Tuesdays.

d. I love going to the .... because they've got a telescope.

e. Zach enjoys silence and quiet. His favourite club is the ....

f. Do you read poems in the ....?

A Are you a scientist? ➪ Manuel, *p. 40*

1 • Listen and link Justin to the correct picture.

JUSTIN

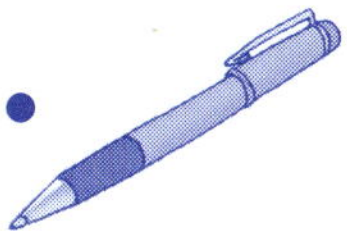

2 • Listen and link the people to their clubs. Link to "?" when you don't know.

Lily	Justin	Alex	Amanda
●	●	●	●
●	●	●	●
?	Science Club	Sign Language Club	Cookery Club

3 • Listen and tick the correct picture.

❑ 

❑ 

4 • Recap.

Justin .... science, but he wants to join the ....

because Amanda ❑ is in the club ❑ isn't in the club.

Conclude.

He ❑ ♥ ❑ (crossed-out ♥) Amanda!

Sam Cooke: *Wonderful World*

➪ Manuel, p. 40

ÉLÈVE 15

1 • Listen and circle the subjects the singer mentions.

history • sports • biology • science • French • English • geography • Spanish • trigonometry • art • algebra

DID YOU KNOW?

La trigonométrie (*trigonometry*) et l'algèbre (*algebra*) font partie des mathématiques. Aux États-Unis, les élèves étudient souvent l'algèbre (étude des nombres et des équations) et la trigonométrie (étude des distances et des angles) dans des cours différents !

2 • Listen again to the song.

a. Use the words you circled to complete the blanks.

b. Which other word is missing?

Don't know much about ....,
Don't know much ....
Don't know much about a .... book,
Don't know much about the .... I took.

But I do know that I .... you,
And I know that if you loved me too,
What a wonderful world this would be.

Don't know much about ....,
Don't know much ....
Don't know much about ....,
Don't know what a slide rule (*) is for.

But I do know that one and one is two,
And if this one could be with you,
What a wonderful world this would be.

Now I don't claim to be an A-student,
But I'm trying to be.
For maybe by being an A-student, baby,
I can win your .... for me.

Don't know much about ....,
Don't know much ....
Don't know much about a .... book,
Don't know much about the .... I took.

But I do know that I .... you,
And I know that if you loved me too,
What a wonderful world this would be.

....
....
.... book
.... I took

But I do know that I .... you,
And I know that if you loved me too,
What a wonderful world this would be.

(*) a slide rule: une règle à calcul.

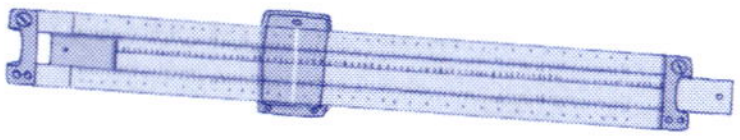

3 • Read the lyrics again and tick the correct answer.

a. Sam Cooke ❑ was ❑ wasn't a very good pupil at school.

b. Sam Cooke's song is about ❑ school ❑ love.

The Music of English

L'accentuation des auxiliaires dans les réponses courtes. ➪ Manuel, *p. 40*

CLASSE CD • 1 31

a. **Écoute les phrases suivantes.**

"Do you like English?"
"Yes, I do."

"Have you got a bike?"
"No, I haven't."

"Is he in the Science Club?"
"No, he isn't."

"Are you fond of animals?"
"Yes, I am."

Dans les réponses courtes, l'auxiliaire ❑ est généralement accentué ❑ n'est pas accentué. C'est pour cela qu'il ne se contracte pas.

CLASSE CD • 1 32

b. **À ton tour, écoute et répète !**

"Do you like me?"
"Yes, I do."

"Have you got a minute?"
"Yes, I have!"

"Can you help me?"
"No, I can't. Ask Tom!"

B The Science Club

➪ Manuel, *p. 41*

1 • Read the questions and then write the number of the correct picture.

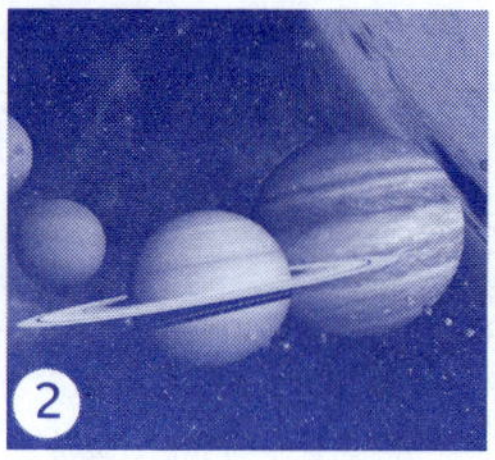

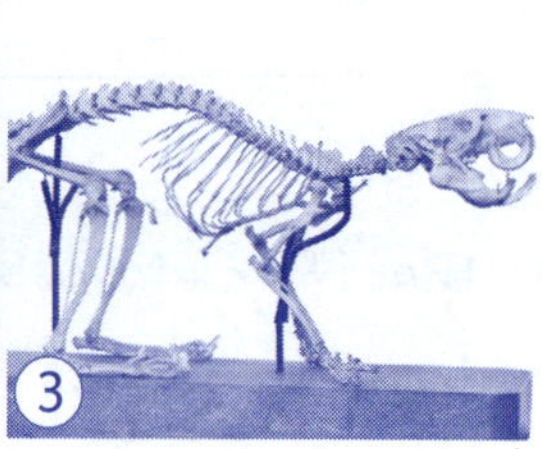

a. Are you crazy about meteors, stars or the mysteries of space travel?
Picture ... ❑ Yes. ❑ No.

b. Is there a telescope on your Christmas list?
Picture ... ❑ Yes. ❑ No.

c. Do you enjoy mixing things and experimenting?
Picture ... ❑ Yes. ❑ No.

d. Do you think skeletons are fun?
Picture ... ❑ Yes. ❑ No.

e. Have you got a collection of fossils or insects under your bed?
Picture ... ❑ Yes. ❑ No.

2 • Answer the questions.

3 • Turn your textbook upside down and count your points.

Are you ready to join the Science Club? ❑ Yes. ❑ No.

4 • Tick the correct answers about the Science Club.

When? ❑ Every day. ❑ Every week. ❑ Every month.
Where? ❑ At Mrs Thomas's house. ❑ At school.

Grammar bag — Les *yes / no questions* et les réponses courtes

Get it.

1. Observe les phrases suivantes.

Have you got a pen?

Yes, I have.

Has Kate got a guitar?

No, she hasn't.

Are you fond of science?

No, I'm not.

Is Tom crazy about meteors?

Yes, he is.

Do you like reading?

No, I don't.

Does Justin love Amanda?

Yes, he does!

2. Encadre les auxiliaires en noir et souligne les sujets en bleu.

3. Relie le sujet de la question à celui de la réponse avec une flèche bleue.

Dans la réponse, le sujet est repris sous la forme d'un .... personnel.

4. Relie l'auxiliaire de la question à celui de la réponse avec une flèche noire.

● Ces questions commencent toutes par ❑ un verbe ❑ un auxiliaire ❑ un sujet.
Ce sont des ***yes / no questions***.
On répond à une ***yes / no question*** par une **réponse courte** :
Yes, ... + ... à la forme affirmative.
No, ... + ... à la forme négative.
L'auxiliaire ❑ s'accorde ❑ ne s'accorde pas avec le sujet.

Remarque :
Dans les réponses courtes, le sujet est repris sous la forme d'un .... personnel.

In the bag.

Écris les réponses courtes.

a. "Has Kelly got a problem?"
"Yes, ..."

b. "Is your father crazy about animals?"
"Yes, ..."

c. "Does he like pancakes?"
"No, ..."

d. "Have you got an idea?"
"No, ..."

e. "Are your friends fond of maths?"
"No, ..."

f. "Do you want to be part of a club?"
"Yes, ..."

You're the actor!

⇨ Manuel, *p. 41*

1 • a. **Work in pairs. Circle a club from the list. You can invent a different one.**
Fashion Club • Dance Club • Band Club • Book Club • Earth Club • Sign Language Club • Games Club • English Club • Cookery Club • Drama Club • ....

b. **On a piece of paper, prepare 5 questions to select the members of your school club.**

Astuces

• Variez les questions.
Are you fond of ...? *Do you enjoy ...?* *Are you interested in ...?*
• N'oubliez pas la terminaison *-ing*, après ces expressions de goût.
*Are you fond of read**ing**?*
• N'oubliez pas de déterminer combien de *yes* ou de *no* sont nécessaires pour s'inscrire dans votre club !

2 • Now write your questions and test 2 friends.

a. ....
Friend 1: ❑ Yes. ❑ No. Friend 2: ❑ Yes. ❑ No.

b. ....
Friend 1: ❑ Yes. ❑ No. Friend 2: ❑ Yes. ❑ No.

c. ....
Friend 1: ❑ Yes. ❑ No. Friend 2: ❑ Yes. ❑ No.

d. ....
Friend 1: ❑ Yes. ❑ No. Friend 2: ❑ Yes. ❑ No.

e. ....
Friend 1: ❑ Yes. ❑ No. Friend 2: ❑ Yes. ❑ No.

Conclude.

❑ One of our friends is ready to join the .... Club.

❑ Our two friends are ready to join the .... Club.

❑ Our friends aren't ready to join the .... Club.

Do you remember?

1 • Écris le nom du club correspondant à chaque dessin.

a

b

c

d

e

f

2 • Associe chaque question à sa réponse.

Are you fond of meteors? •	• No, they haven't.
Does Matt enjoy listening to classical music? •	• No, she isn't.
Have they got a telescope? •	• Yes, I am.
Is your cousin a musician? •	• Yes, they do.
Do scientists like maths? •	• No, he doesn't.

3 • Réponds aux questions en utilisant des réponses courtes.

a. Have you got any pets? → ....

b. Are you interested in astronomy? → ....

c. Do you have maths on Monday mornings? → ....

d. Is it sunny today? → ....

e. Is your best friend in your class? → ....

CULTURE CORNER British ... or American?

➪ Manuel, pp. 44-45

A Play the culture game.

Draw a yellow cab.

B Words!

Complete with the correct answer.

1. What is the other word for "cab"? ....
2. The British word for "cookie" is "............................" .
3. The Americans say "............................" for "chips".
4. The American word for "rubber" is "............................".
5. The Americans say "............................" for "sweets".

Did you know?

American and British governments

1. What's wrong? Read the sentences and correct the mistakes.

In the United Kingdom:

a. The Queen lives at 10 Downing Street, London.

....

b. When the Prime Minister is at home, we can see the royal flag on top of his house.

....

In the United States:

c. The White House is in New York.

....

d. The President's office is round.

....

e. The First Lady's offices are in the West Wing.

....

2. Write the captions under the photos.

....

....

The Spotlight

A new pet

➪ Manuel, *p. 46*

Do you remember the video?

Write captions or fill in the balloons.

PART 1

PART 2

CHECK YOUR PROGRESS

☹ 😐 ☺

MON GUIDE D'AUTO-ÉVALUATION

➩ **Manuel**, *p. 48*

Vocabulary challenge

Can you find the twenty words from the workshop?

Tu as trouvé • moins de 6 mots ☹ • de 7 à 11 mots 😐 • plus de 11 mots ☺.

Down

1. After dinner, you ... the table.
2. When you clean a carpet, you ...
3. You can ... a bike or a horse.
4. Before dinner, you ... the table.
5. Synonym for "practise".
6. When you like clothes, you're fond of ...
7. American people like ... syrup on their pancakes.
8. When your room is messy, you must ... it.
9. A horse can jump it.
10. 60 minutes.
11. I ... my bed every morning.
12. All the days of the week.

Across

2. Someone who often helps is ...
4. 
9. A document that gives information about a club for example.
13. The name of the planet where we live.
14. A group of musicians.
15. Opposite of hard-working.
16. The things you must do at home.
17. A little dog.

1. Check your vocabulary.

Tu as trouvé • moins de 3 mots ☹ • de 4 à 6 mots 😐 • plus de 6 mots ☺.

2. Check your tools.

a. What do they like doing?

Tu as utilisé
- moins de 2 verbes ou expressions de goûts. ☹
- 3 verbes ou expressions de goût. 😐
- au moins 4 verbes ou expressions de goût. ☺

Ces verbes étaient suivis de BV-*ing*. • Jamais. ☹ • Parfois. 😐 • Toujours. ☺

b. Find adjectives to describe their personalities.

Tu as trouvé
- un adjectif ☹
- 2 ou 3 adjectifs 😐
- au moins 4 adjectifs. ☺

c. Imagine what they often do or never do.

Tu as mis un -*s* aux verbes à la 3ᵉ personne du singulier.
- Rarement. ☹ • Souvent. 😐 • Toujours. ☺

Tu as utilisé
- 2 adverbes et expressions de fréquence. ☹
- 3 adverbes et expressions de fréquence. 😐
- au moins 4 adverbes et expressions de fréquence. ☺

Tu as correctement placé les adverbes.
- Rarement. ☹ • Souvent. 😐 • Toujours. ☺

d. Choose one character and ask five yes / no questions. Imagine his / her answers.

Tu as réussi
- moins de 2 *yes / no questions* ☹
- 3 *yes / no questions* 😐
- au moins 4 *yes / no questions*. ☺

Tu as réussi
- moins de 2 réponses courtes ☹
- 3 réponses courtes 😐
- au moins 4 réponses courtes. ☺

Quand tu as entouré ☹ ou 😐, révise le point concerné :

2. a. ➪ Manuel, *p. 38* **: Exprimer ses goûts.**

2. b. ➪ Words, *p. 32*

2. c. ➪ Manuel, *p. 34* **: Parler de ses habitudes.**

➪ Manuel, *p. 34* **: L'expression de la fréquence.**

2. d. ➪ Manuel, *p. 42* **: Les *yes / no questions* et les réponses courtes.**

New horizons

TAKE 1 *New friends at school*

Warm up. ➪ Manuel, *p. 50*

1. After listening, write the nationality for each name.

2. Then link the names to their flags and colour them in.

Astuce

As-tu bien mis les majuscules aux adjectifs de nationalité ? Relis et vérifie.

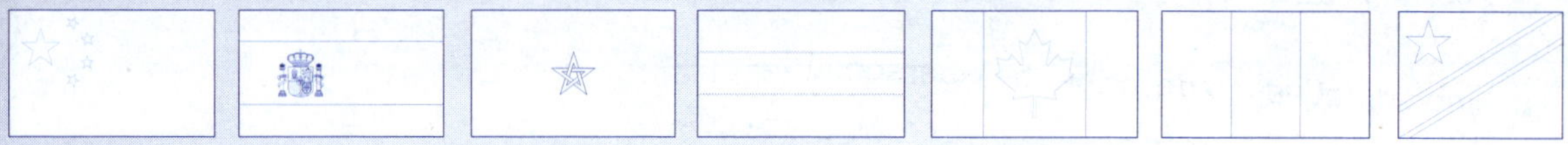

•	•	•	•	•	•	•
•	•	•	•	•	•	•
Juan	Adrian	Sara	Lian	Mason	Kya	Alani
....	....	....	....	....	....	....

A New pupils ➪ Manuel, *p. 50*

1 • Listen and tick the correct answer.

It's ❑ before school ❑ at school ❑ after school.

2 • The new girl: Listen and give the correct answer.

a. She's in .... and ....'s class.

b. Name: .... Nationality: ....

c. Her family arrived last ....

d. She ❑ ♥ ❑ 💔 the school in Largo.

e. Her school was ❑ different ❑ not different.

f. Number of pupils in her class: ....

Number of teachers in her class: ....

Astuces

- La terminaison *-ese* de *Congolese* est toujours accentuée. Ex. : *Portugu**ese**, Senegal**ese*** ...
- Quand les adjectifs se terminent par *-an*, c'est l'avant-dernière syllabe qui est accentuée. Ex. : ***Ita**lian, **Ger**man, Mo**roc**can* ...

Astuce

Last, pour dire « dernier », se place **avant** le nom en anglais.
lundi ***dernier*** → ***last*** *Monday*

3 • The new boy: Listen and give the correct answer.

a. He's in ....'s class.

b. Name: .... Nationality : ....

c. Number the pictures in the right order and cross the odd one out.

☐ 

☐ 

☐ 

4 • Recap.

There were .... new pupils at school today. The boy, Patrick, is .... and the girl, Binta, is ....

Patrick was ❏ shy ❏ impressed ❏ happy.

Binta was ❏ angry ❏ surprised ❏ sad.

Conclude.

❏ Lily liked Patrick very much. ❏ Lily didn't really like Patrick.

Grammar bag Le prétérit (1) : la forme affirmative de *be*, *have* et des verbes réguliers

Get it.

1. Observe les phrases suivantes.

It was difficult.

They had one teacher.

The kids were new.

Binta arrived last week.

2. Complète le tableau ci-dessous.

	Verbe *be*	Verbe *have (got)*	Verbes réguliers
Forme au prétérit	.... /	....	BV + ...
Exemples	*I .... late yesterday.* *My friends .... at home last weekend.*	*I .... a problem this morning.*	*She visit..... the school this morning.*

Rappels

- ***Am*** et ***is*** deviennent .... au prétérit alors que ***are*** devient ....
- .... disparaît lorsque ***have got*** est au prétérit.
- Les verbes **réguliers** prennent -........ à toutes les personnes.

Attention !
Les verbes d'une syllabe se terminant par une consonne précédée d'une seule voyelle doublent la consonne. Ex. : *sto**p*** → *sto**pp**ed*

In the bag.

Mets les phrases suivantes au prétérit.

a. I'm at home. On Monday, ...

b. John chats in class. Yesterday, ...

c. My father's tired. .... this morning!

d. The dogs are in the garden. .... at 2.30 pm.

e. They invite our family for Thanksgiving.
Last year, ...

f. I've got a problem with my mobile.
.... this afternoon.

The Music of English

La prononciation du -*ed*. ⇨ Manuel, *p. 50*

CLASSE CD • 1 39

a. **Écoute les verbes suivants et coche les sons que tu entends.**

	played	jumped	wanted	dropped	escaped	called
/d/						
/t/						
/ɪd/						

Attention !
La terminaison -*ed* ne se prononce jamais /ed/. Elle se prononce :
– /t/ après les sons /f/, /k/, /p/, /s/ et /tʃ/ ;
– /ɪd/ après les sons /t/ et /d/ ;
– /d/ dans les autres cas.

b. **Faites trois trains (un par prononciation de la terminaison -*ed*) à afficher dans la classe, comme illustré ci-dessous.**

B World Dances Club ➪ Manuel, *p. 51*

1 • This afternoon Lily went to ...

☐ the Science Club ☐ the World Dances Club ☐ the Cookery Club.

2 • Link the children to their activities.

Binta • Patrick •

• 

• 

• 

3 • Who was Patrick's teacher?

☐ His sister. ☐ His mother. ☐ His grandmother.

4 • Tick the correct picture.

☐ 

☐ 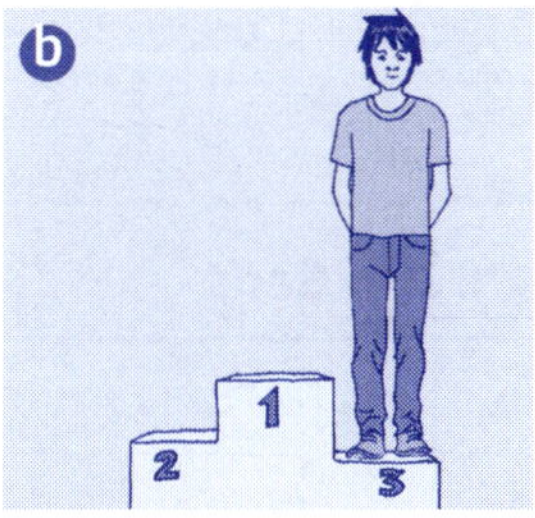

☐ 

5 • Number the pictures in the right order.

☐ 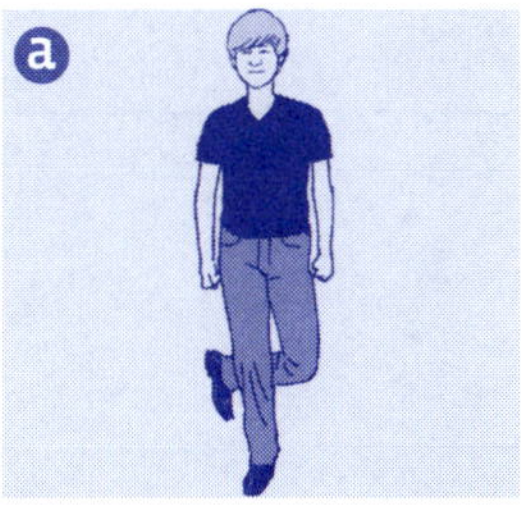

☐ 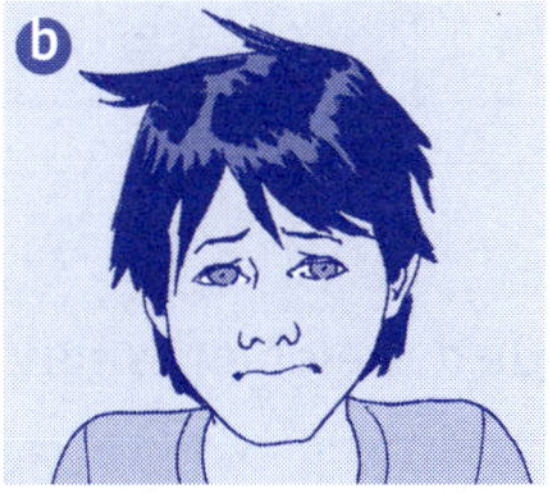

☐ 

☐ 

☐ 

6 • Recap.

Binta and Patrick .... and .... this morning in the World Dances Club.

Justin tried to dance, but he .... The pupils .... and Justin was very embarrassed when Amanda ....

Conclude: Circle the expressions that correspond to Justin.

shy jealous honest respectful in love

Grammar bag — Le prétérit (1) : la forme affirmative des verbes irréguliers

Get it.

1. Observe les phrases suivantes.

I went to the club. *Amanda came into the room.* *He fell on the floor.*

2. Souligne les sujets en bleu et encadre les verbes en rouge.

Les verbes ci-dessus sont ❑ réguliers ❑ irréguliers.

● On ne peut pas deviner le prétérit des verbes irréguliers. Il faut l'apprendre ....

⇨ Verbes irréguliers, Manuel p. 191

Le verbe au prétérit ❑ change ❑ ne change pas de forme en fonction du **sujet**.

3. Complète les tableaux ci-dessous.

Sens	Base verbale	Prétérit
prendre	....	....
enseigner	....	....
venir	....	....
aller	....	....

Sens	Base verbale	Prétérit
faire	....	....
gagner	....	....
tomber	....	....
chanter	....	....

In the bag.

Construis des phrases au prétérit à l'aide des éléments suivants.

a. John / to the cinema / yesterday / go / .

....

b. the violin / teach / him / his mother / he / and / win / a prize / .

....

c. to the concert / my parents / they / photos / come / and / take / .

....

Take your pen.

Raconte ce que Steven et son ami ont fait samedi dernier en te servant des images.
Tu peux utiliser les verbes suivants : *go • go back • fall • win • teach • be.*

....

....

....

....

....

....

You're the actor!

➪ Manuel, *p. 51*

Pupil A: Prepare your story.

When? Last ....

Your friend's nationality: ....

Activity: ....

....

Astuce

Pense à ajouter des détails pour rendre ton histoire plus intéressante (les sentiments, le moment de la journée, le lieu...).

Do you remember?

1 • Retrouve les nationalités suivantes.

a. ANDCAAIN → ....

b. MANGER → ....

c. GLOCENOSE → ....

d. RISIH → ....

e. PANSSIH → ....

f. CROMACON → ....

g. NICHEES → ....

2 • Réécris les phrases suivantes en mettant les verbes au prétérit.

a. Patrick is shy. → .... in front of the class.

b. He dances very well. → .... this morning.

c. Patrick comes back from Ireland. → .... last week.

d. His parents are in Ireland. → Last month, ...

**3 • Colorie les 10 verbes irréguliers en jaune et les 6 verbes réguliers en vert.
Écris la forme des prétérits irréguliers à côté de la grille.**

F	H	A	V	E	M	Q	N	N	I
I	F	R	G	T	T	E	A	C	H
H	S	O	F	R	U	V	T	W	B
W	I	N	A	A	R	R	I	V	E
W	N	C	L	X	O	T	N	K	E
D	G	N	L	D	F	K	A	S	P
A	W	T	A	L	K	C	R	K	X
N	K	S	O	B	L	U	S	H	E
C	C	O	M	E	V	I	S	I	T
E	N	L	A	U	G	H	D	H	T

Base verbale	→	Prétérit
....	→	....
....	→	....
....	→	....
....	→	....
....	→	....
....	→	....
....	→	....
....	→	....
....	→	....
....	→	....

TAKE 2 *Families!*

I CAN *do it!*

➪ Manuel, *p. 35*

> Comment apprendre mon vocabulaire ?
Regroupe les mots liés à ***family*** dans un soleil de mots.

ÉLÈVE ROM ➪ *My picture dictionary*

Warm up. ➪ Manuel, *p. 54*

Complete the crossword with the right words.

Across

1. Your brother is your father's ...
2. She's your aunt's daughter.
3. He's your mother's brother.
4. Your sister is your father's ...

Down

5. Your uncle is your aunt's ...
6. You're an ... child if you haven't got any brothers or sisters.
7. She's your father's wife.
8. She's your mother's sister.

A A family tree

➪ Manuel, p. 54

1 • Listen and say where the scene takes place.

❑ At the Browns'. ❑ At the Millers'.

2 • Listen and tick who's present.

❑ Shannon. ❑ Mary.
❑ The twins. ❑ Lily.

I CAN do it!

➪ Manuel, p. 53

> Comment bien comprendre un document oral (1) ?

Pour comprendre **la situation**, appuie-toi sur **les bruitages** et les **intonations** !

Que se passe-t-il au tout début ? On entend

....

Qui ouvre la porte ? ....

Les personnages sont-ils ❑ contents ❑ contrariés ?

3 • Complete the information about Shannon's great-grandfather.

Name: ....
Nationality: ....
Date of birth: ....
Place of birth: ....
Job: ....
Date of emigration: ....

4 • Tick the picture corresponding to Shannon's ancestor's life in the USA. Write "?" when you don't know.

a

❑

b

❑

c

❑

5 • Recap.

Shannon's ancestors .... to the USA because they were ....
They bought .... in the West.

Conclude.

Justin is ❑ very interested in ❑ bored with the conversation.

Grammar bag — Le prétérit (2) : la forme interrogative et les réponses courtes

Get it.

■ Les questions et réponses courtes avec *be*.

1. Observe les phrases suivantes.

"Was Patrick Irish?"
"Yes, he was."

"Was he a farmer?"
"No, he wasn't."

"Were his ancestors from Ireland?"
"Yes, they were."

"Were they poor?"
"No, they weren't."

2. Entoure les verbes en rouge et souligne les sujets en bleu.

● Pour poser une question au prétérit avec le verbe ***be***, on inverse le .... et le .... ***Be*** ❑ s'accorde ❑ ne s'accorde pas avec le sujet.
● Dans les réponses courtes, on reprend le .... (sous forme de pronom personnel) suivi de l'auxiliaire ....

■ Les questions et réponses courtes avec les autres verbes.

3. Observe les phrases suivantes.

"Did they emigrate to the USA?"
"Yes, they did."

"Did they buy a farm?"
"No, they didn't."

4. Entoure le verbe en rouge, souligne le sujet en bleu et encadre l'auxiliaire en noir.

● Avec les autres verbes, on utilise l'auxiliaire .... dans les questions au prétérit. Le verbe est à la ....
● Dans les réponses courtes, on reprend le .... (sous forme de pronom personnel) suivi de l'auxiliaire ....

In the bag.

1 Relie les questions aux réponses courtes qui leur correspondent.

Did John buy a new car? ●	● Yes, they were.
Was your father happy? ●	● No, he wasn't.
Were your friends at home yesterday? ●	● Yes, I was.
Did the cats eat the cake? ●	● Yes, he did.
Were you tired this morning? ●	● No, they didn't.

2 Réponds aux questions à l'aide de réponses courtes.

a. "Did your parents eat at home?" "No, ..."
b. "Was their dog nice?" "Yes, it ...."
c. "Did Mary call you last night?" "Yes, ..."
d. "Were your ancestors poor?" "No, ..."

The Music of English

La prononciation de *was* et de *wasn't*. ➪ Manuel, *p. 54*

CLASSE CD • 1 46

a. **Écoute les phrases suivantes.**

He was born in June. *When was she born?* *I wasn't tired*

"Was he happy?" *"Yes, he was."*

Souligne *was* ou *wasn't* lorsqu'ils sont accentués.

Was est accentué lorsqu'il est ❑ en début de phrase ❑ en fin de phrase ❑ tout le temps.

Lorsque ***was*** n'est pas accentué, sa voyelle se prononce /ə/.

Remarque : *wasn't* est toujours accentué. Sa voyelle se prononce en général /ɒ/ comme dans ***dog***.

CLASSE CD • 1 47

b. **Dis les phrases suivantes à voix haute puis écoute et vérifie.**

"Where was he yesterday? He wasn't at school."

"He was at home. He was sick."

"Oh, really?"

"Yes, he was."

B An Irish song

➪ Manuel, *p. 55*

1 • What did Shannon's grandfather play?

❑ The guitar. ❑ The piano. ❑ The fiddle.

2 • Listen to the song and complete the lyrics.

ÉLÈVE • 19

CLASSE CD • 1 49

♫ Pat lived in Dublin with his ....
Oh, poor Pat, he didn't have ....
He gave a rose to his sweet Molly
And left .... for a new ....

♫ Goodbye Ireland, goodbye to you.
My home is here, but I must go.
Goodbye Ireland, goodbye Molly.
I love you two, but I must go.

3 • Recap: Circle the correct answers.

Shannon's grandfather was a cowboy / a musician. He wrote a song about Pat.
Pat was Irish / American and he went to the USA because he had / he didn't have any money in Ireland.

Conclude.

A lot of Americans have Irish ...., so Irish music is very popular in the USA.

Grammar bag — Le prétérit (3) : la forme négative

Get it.

1. Observe les phrases suivantes.

He wasn't rich. *They weren't farmers.*

They didn't buy a farm. *She didn't emigrate to the USA.*

2. Entoure les verbes en rouge. Puis, encadre les auxiliaires en noir et souligne les négations en vert.

- Avec le verbe ***be***, on n'utilise pas l'auxiliaire .... à la forme négative : c'est .... qui porte la négation.
- Avec les autres verbes, on utilise l'auxiliaire .... à la forme négative devant le verbe
❑ au prétérit ❑ à la base verbale.

In the bag.

Mets les phrases suivantes à la forme négative.

a. He was sick yesterday. → ....

b. They bought a big farm. → ....

c. They were Irish. → ....

d. They emigrated in 1850. → ....

Take your pen.

Tu as rencontré Mrs Blake. Elle a écrit la biographie de son ancêtre irlandaise qui avait ouvert une célèbre école de danse à New York.

Prépare 5 questions à lui poser pour en savoir plus sur son ancêtre, Jane O'Hara.

1. ....?
2. ....?
3. ....?
4. ....?
5. ....?

Astuce

Varie tes questions en utilisant des mots interrogatifs différents : *When ...? Why ...?* Etc.
➪ Se renseigner, Manuel, p. 167.
Utilise aussi des *yes / no questions* : *Did she ...?* *Was she ...?*

You're the actor! ➪ Manuel, *p. 55*

Complete your ancestor's card.

MY ANCESTOR

My ancestor is number ....
Name: ....
Date of birth: ....
Family relationship: ....
Hobby / Job: ....
❑ very poor ❑ poor ❑ rich ❑ very rich

I CAN do it!

➪ Manuel, *p. 39*

> Comment prendre la parole en anglais? (1)

Quand tu n'es pas sûr(e) d'avoir bien compris : *Sorry, can you say that again?*

Complete your classmate's ancestor's card.

MY CLASSMATE'S ANCESTOR

Name: ....
Date of birth: ....
Family relationship: ....
Hobby / Job: ....
❑ very poor ❑ poor ❑ rich ❑ very rich
My classmate's ancestor is number ....

Do you remember?

1 • Complète les lettres manquantes pour retrouver les liens de parenté.

a. F A _ _ _ _
b. A U _ _
c. H U S _ _ _ _
d. U N _ _ _
e. D A U _ _ _ _ _
f. W _ _ _

2 • Écris le mot correspondant à la définition.

a. He's the father of your father. He's your ....
b. She's your mother's sister. She's your ....
c. He's your mother's husband. He's your ....
d. His wife is your aunt. He's your ....

3 • Écris les contraires des adjectifs suivants.

a. easy ≠ .... b. expensive ≠ .... c. rich ≠ ....

4 • Remets les éléments dans l'ordre pour former une phrase correcte et barre l'intrus.

a. buy / bought / your parents / did / when / their new car / ?

....

b. Walter / visit / visited / last year / did / Ireland / ?

....

c. in 1932 / weren't / didn't / very rich / my ancestors / .

....

d. land / in 1940 / cheap / in the West / was / did / ?

....

e. leave / left / London / we / didn't / last summer / .

....

TAKE 3 *Success stories*

Warm up. ➪ Manuel, *p. 58*

Complete the mystery words.

a. It's a synonym for "be in a film". → a.........

b. Penelope Cruz is a famous Spanish a.................. .

c. A d.................... makes films.

d. If a film has a lot of success, it's s......................... .

e. A s............... film is a film without dialogue, usually in black and white.

Astuce

Attention : *Library* est un faux ami car il signifie
....
C'est le mot *bookshop* qui veut dire « librairie » !

A At the library ➪ Manuel, *p. 58*

1 • Listen and tick the correct answer.

a. Justin and Alex are ❑ in a bookshop ❑ at the library.

b. They're ❑ happy ❑ irritated because ❑ they can find what they want.
❑ they can't find anything.

2 • Listen and circle the correct answers.

a. They want some information about George Clooney / Charlie Chaplin / Levi Strauss.

b. They want a biography / a history book / a magazine / a DVD.

c. He was an American actor and director / a British actor and director.

d. He emigrated to the USA / to Australia when he was young.

e. Miss Ferguson has some DVD boxes and some books / nothing about him in her library.

3 • Recap: Complete the text.

Justin and Alex wanted .... information about Charlie Chaplin, but they didn't find .... about him in the library. Miss Ferguson helped them because she knew she had .... about him.

Conclude.

Alex and Justin are ❑ embarrassed ❑ proud because they didn't know Charlie Chaplin wasn't ❑ American ❑ British.

The Music of English

L'accentuation des composés de *some*, *any* et *no*. ⇨ Manuel, p. 58

CLASSE CD • 1 52

a. **Écoute les phrases suivantes. Puis, souligne la syllabe accentuée dans *something*, *anything* et *nothing*.**

I don't know anything about him.
There's nothing in this article!
I learned something interesting today.
Did you see anything?

Dans les composés *something*, *anything* et *nothing*, c'est ❑ *-thing* ❑ la première syllabe qui est accentué(e).

CLASSE CD • 1 53

b. **Dis les phrases suivantes à voix haute puis écoute et vérifie.**

"Did you see anything?" *"Yes, I saw something!"*
"I didn't see anything!" *"We saw nothing!"*

"Did you buy anything?" *"Yes, I bought something!"*
"I didn't buy anything!" *"We bought nothing!"*

c. **À ton tour de faire d'autres phrases sur ce modèle.**

Grammar bag — *Some, any, no* et leurs composés en *-thing*

Get it.

■ *Some, any* et *no*.

1. Observe les phrases suivantes.

Have you got ***any*** *Irish ancestors?* .....
There aren't ***any*** *German pupils in my class.* .....
They had ***some*** *money.* .....
But they had ***no*** *car!* .....

Some et ***any*** indiquent une quantité ❑ précise ❑ imprécise.

2. Note sur les pointillés s'il s'agit d'une phrase affirmative (A), négative (N) ou interrogative (I).

3. Souligne en rouge les phrases qui parlent de l'absence de quelque chose.
On utilise soit .... dans une phrase affirmative soit .... dans une phrase négative.

● ***Some*** s'emploie dans les phrases .... alors que ***any*** s'emploie dans les phrases .... ou ....

● Pour parler de l'absence de quelque chose, on utilise .... dans une phrase **négative** ou .... dans une phrase **affirmative**.

Remarque : *Some* et ***any*** sont souvent utilisés comme **pronoms** pour éviter les répétitions.
"Have you got any biscuits?" *"Yes, we've got* ***some****."* *"No, we haven't got* ***any****."*

■ Les composés de *some, any* et *no*.

● ***Something*** (« quelque chose »), ***anything*** (« quelque chose » dans les questions, « rien » dans les phrases négatives) et ***nothing*** (« rien ») s'utilisent selon les mêmes règles.

In the bag.

1 Choisis entre *some, any* et *no*.
"I've got .... milk and .... biscuits, but have you got .... coffee?"
"No, I'm afraid we haven't got .... and we've got .... tea."

2 Mets la phrase à la forme négative de deux façons différentes.
a. There are some girls in our group.
....
b. We have got some money.
....

3 Entoure la bonne réponse.
"I'm hungry. Is there something / anything / nothing in the fridge?"
"Sorry, I've got something / anything / nothing to eat and I haven't got something / anything / nothing to drink!"

B Charlie Chaplin

➪ Manuel, *p. 59*

Document 1

1 • Read Document 1 in your textbook and tick the correct answers.

a. Justin often posts messages on the forum. ❑ Right. ❑ Wrong.

b. How long ago did Justin post his message?................................ .

It's Saturday, 1 pm: what time did he write his message? ❑ At 9 am. ❑ At 10 am. ❑ At 11 am.

c. When did he watch *The Gold Rush*? ❑ On Friday night. ❑ On Thursday night.

d. Which scene did Justin prefer?

1  ❑

2  ❑

2 • Read this passage again.

Blog post: 1 — Posted 3 hours ago

I can't believe that only 24 hours ago I knew nothing about Charlie Chaplin. Does anyone know how long ago he created this character and why?

a. Underline the expression showing that Justin discovered Chaplin yesterday.

b. Circle the expression showing that Justin wants to know when Chaplin created this character.

Document 2

3 • Read the first two paragraphs and complete Chaplin's timeline.

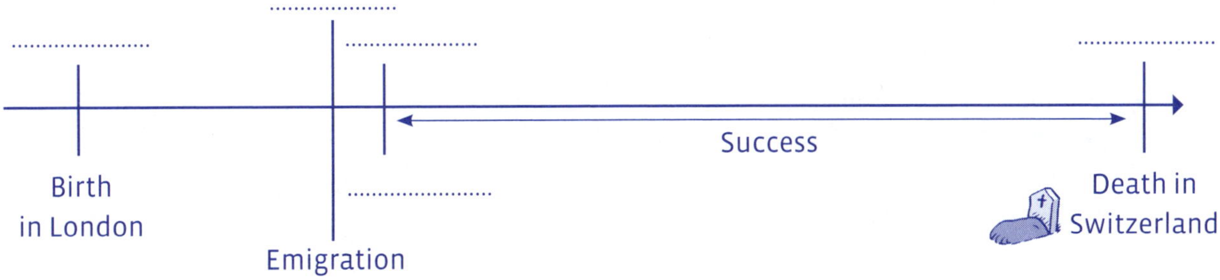

4 • Read the biography and tick the correct answers.

a. Charlie Chaplin invented this character ❑ between 1905 and 1910.
❑ between 1914 and 1920.
❑ in 1978.

b. He invented this look because ❑ he didn't like his clothes for a film.
❑ he had an accident with his costume.

c. Size 14 shoes are ❑ very small ❑ very big.

DID YOU KNOW?

Le système des pointures est très différent aux États-Unis.
Le 14 correspond environ au 48 dans le système français !

5 • Recap: Circle the correct answer.

About 50 / 100 years ago, Charlie Chaplin created a new character, the Tramp.

Chaplin became / didn't become very famous with this character.

Conclude.

Charlie Chaplin created

❑ a funny character ❑ a serious character.

I CAN do it !

➩ **Manuel,** *p. 57*

> Comment apprendre mes verbes irréguliers ?
Complète ton jeu de cartes avec *become*.

Astuce

Pour dire « il y a » dans une **expression de temps**, on utilise le mot ***ago*** que l'on place après l'indication de durée.

*I saw him two days **ago**.*

Attention : Ne confonds pas avec l'expression « il y a » pour affirmer **l'existence** de quelque chose.

***There is** a computer in my bedroom.*
***There are** books in my bag.*

Do you remember?

Astuce

Entraîne-toi à dire les mots tout haut pour bien mémoriser leur prononciation.

1 • Lis la liste de mots ci-dessous.

silent • famous • act • successful

a. Souligne les adjectifs et entoure leur syllabe accentuée.

b. Comment dit-on « films muets » ? ....

2 • Écris les mots correspondant aux définitions.

a. A woman who acts in a film. → ....

b. A person in a film → ....

c. A hundred years → ....

d. Write on a forum → ....

3 • Complète avec *some*, *any*, ou *no*.

"Are there .... books about silent films, Miss?"

"Yes, there are .... here, on the top shelf. But we've got .... books about Charlie Chaplin at the moment."

4 • Complète avec *something*, *anything* ou *nothing*.

Today was a horrible day! First, I watched a French film and I didn't understand ....!
Then, I went for a walk. But there was .... in my shoe and I had a terrible time.
Finally, I went home. I was very hungry, but there was .... for dinner in the fridge.

5 • Nous sommes le 17 novembre. Lis l'agenda ci-dessous et explique de quelle façon Will a préparé l'anniversaire de son amie Alice en utilisant *ago*.

NOVEMBER							
1		8		15	*flower shop*	22	
2		9		16		23	
3	*write invitations*	10	*find present*	17	*Alice's birthday party!*	24	
4		11		18		25	
5		12		19		26	
6		13		20		27	
7		14	*buy birthday card*	21		28	

....

....

....

....

The Spotlight

Christmas dinner

➩ Manuel, p. 62

Do you remember the video?

Write captions or fill in the balloons.

PART 1

PART 2

Oh! Granny bought ....

PROJECT

➩ Manuel, p. 63

This is my ancestor

Prepare your story.

Astuce

Pour rendre ton histoire plus amusante et plus intéressante, ajoute des **détails** : description physique, lieu du mariage, météo, invités, moyen de transport pour l'arrivée dans le pays, depuis combien de temps...

Origin and destination	Family life	Event	Job

CHECK YOUR PROGRESS ☹ 😐 ☺

MON GUIDE D'AUTO-ÉVALUATION ➪ Manuel, *p. 64*

Vocabulary challenge

Can you find the eighteen words from the workshop?

Tu as trouvé • moins de 6 mots ☹ • de 7 à 11 mots 😐 • plus de 11 mots ☺.

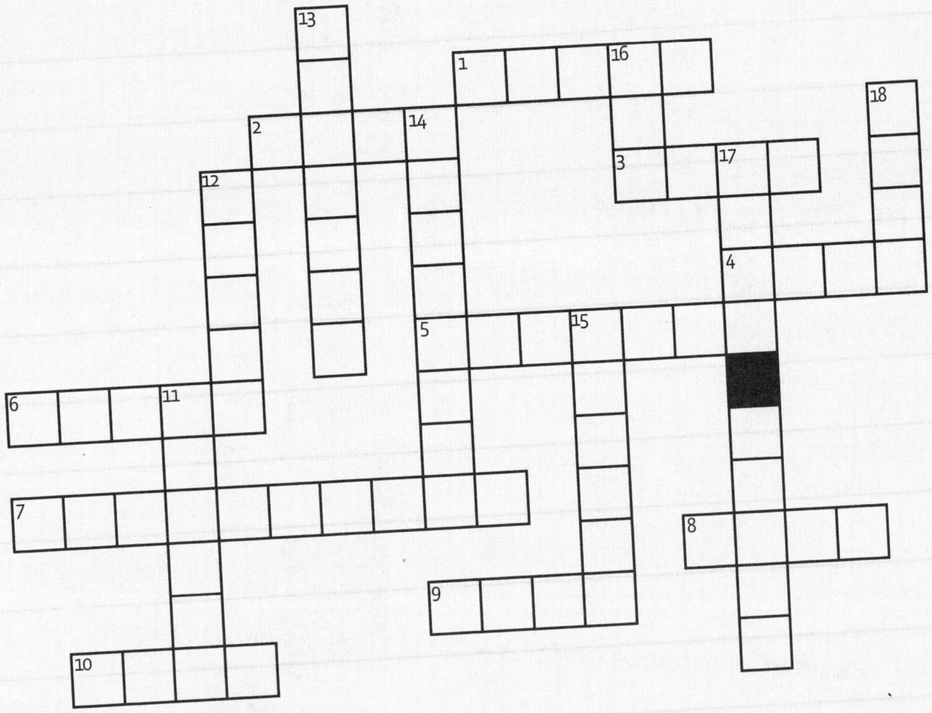

Across

1. Opposite of "expensive".
2. Difficult.
3. Preterite of "take".
4. Preterite of "leave".
5. 100 years.
6. You ... when something is very funny.
7. The people in a book.
8. Opposite of "poor".
9. Write on a forum.
10. Preterite of "go".

Down

11. From Berlin.
12. When you become red, you ...
13. From Madrid.
14. He makes films.
15. Preterite of "teach".
16. Play a role.
17. When you have no brothers or sisters.
18. My uncle's wife is my ...

1. Check your vocabulary.

Tu as trouvé • moins de 3 mots ☹ • de 4 à 6 mots 😐 • plus de 6 mots ☺.

2. Check your tools.

a. What did they do? Say how long ago they did it.

Tu as utilisé correctement
- moins de 2 verbes réguliers et irréguliers. ☹
- de 4 à 6 verbes réguliers et irréguliers. 😐
- plus de 6 verbes réguliers et irréguliers. ☺

Tu as employé les expressions *ago* et *last*.
- Jamais. ☹ • Une fois. 😐 • Plusieurs fois. ☺

b. Ask Kate three yes / no questions. Imagine her answers.

Tes *yes / no questions* étaient correctes. • Jamais. ☹ • Parfois. 😐 • Toujours. ☺

Tes réponses courtes étaient correctes. • Jamais. ☹ • Parfois. 😐 • Toujours. ☺

Tu as utilisé *anything* dans au moins une question. • Oui. ☺ • Non. ☹

Tu as utilisé *something* dans au moins une réponse. • Oui. ☺ • Non. ☹

Quand tu as entouré ☹ ou 😐, révise le point concerné :

2. a. ⇨ Manuel, *p. 52* **: Raconter un événement au passé.**

⇨ Manuel, *p. 60* **: Dater un événement avec *ago*.**

2. b. ⇨ Manuel, *p. 56* **: Échanger des informations sur un événement passé.**

England!

TAKE 1 Holidays in Canterbury

Warm up. ➪ Manuel, p. 66

Label these pictures with the correct word or expression.

gloves / half mittens • winter coat • scarf • sweater • rubber boots • raincoat

....

....

....
....

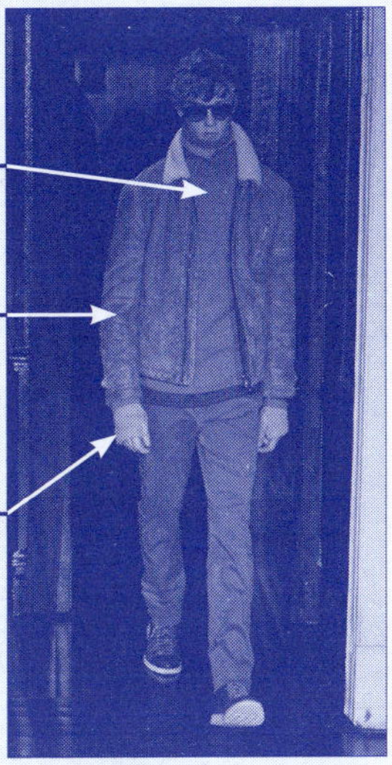

....

....

....

A What's going on? ➪ Manuel, p. 66

1 • What are they doing? Where are they? Link the elements of the three columns.

Lily • •  • • living-room

Mr Brown • • 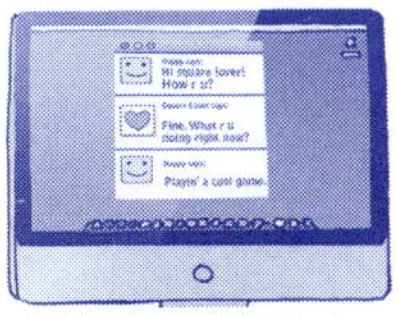 •

Alex • • 

• • bedroom

2 • Circle what Mr Brown's got and cross the odd one out.

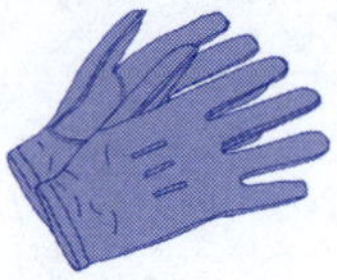

3 • Tick the correct answers.

a. The children are ❑ curious ❑ angry.

b. Justin says: ❑ I want it! ❑ I've got it! ❑ I know it!
because he ❑ understands ❑ doesn't understand what is in his mother's envelope.

4 • What's in the envelope?

❑ 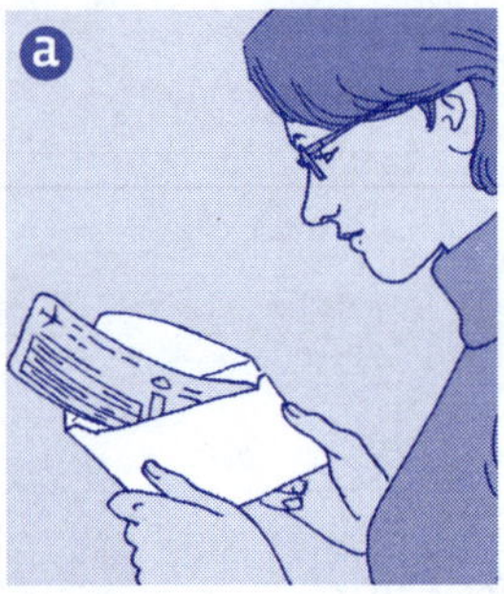

❑ 

❑ 

5 • Recap.

Mr Brown .... his suitcase because he .... for England tomorrow.

Conclude: Tick the correct answers.

❑ All the family's going to England tomorrow.

❑ Mr Brown's going to England tomorrow.

❑ Mr Brown's going to England next week.

❑ The rest of the family's going to England next week.

Grammar bag — Le présent en *be* + BV-*ing*

Get it.

1. Observe les phrases suivantes.

a. *"What are you doing?"*

"I'm packing."

b. *"Where is he going tomorrow?"*

"He's going to England!"

2. Souligne les sujets en bleu, encadre les auxiliaires en noir et les verbes en rouge.

Les phrases du dialogue **a.** décrivent ❑ une action habituelle ❑ une action en cours ❑ une action prévue.

Les phrases du dialogue **b.** décrivent ❑ une action habituelle ❑ une action en cours ❑ une action prévue.

● Pour décrire une action .... ou ...., on utilise le présent en ***be* + BV-*ing***.
Il se conjugue avec l'auxiliaire .... et le verbe auquel on ajoute la terminaison ....
Pour parler d'actions prévues, on ajoute souvent un marqueur de temps comme .... ou ....

● ***Be*** ❑ s'accorde ❑ ne s'accorde pas avec le sujet.

● Dans les questions, on inverse le .... et l'.................................. .

● Dans les formes négatives, c'est l'auxiliaire .... qui porte la négation.
Ex. : He is............ sleeping!

Attention !
Lorsqu'un verbe se termine par un -*e*, on enlève le -*e* avant d'ajouter la terminaison -*ing*.
*Ex. : We dance. → We're dan**cing**.*

In the bag.

Construis les phrases suivantes à l'aide des éléments proposés et indique si l'action est en cours ou prévue.

a. Where's John? What .... he .... *(do)*? ❑ action en cours ❑ action prévue

b. He .... *(read)* in the garden. ❑ action en cours ❑ action prévue

c. I .... *(go)* to the cinema this afternoon. ❑ action en cours ❑ action prévue

d. What .... we .... *(do)* next weekend? ❑ action en cours ❑ action prévue

e. I .... *(not go out)* this afternoon. ❑ action en cours ❑ action prévue

f. Look! It .... *(rain)*. ❑ action en cours ❑ action prévue

The Music of English

L'accentuation des mots porteurs de sens. ➪ Manuel, p. 66

CLASSE CD • 2 03

a. **Écoute les phrases suivantes.**

He's going to school at eight. *What are they doing?* *She's wearing a blue scarf.*

b. **Entoure les mots les plus accentués dans la phrase.**

Ces mots sont dits plus fort car ce sont des mots **importants**. Ils permettent de comprendre le **sens** de la phrase. À l'écoute, appuie-toi sur eux, ils t'aideront à comprendre l'essentiel.

Remarque : Les mots grammaticaux comme les déterminants (*the, my, a* ...), les prépositions (*on, in, at* ...), les auxiliaires (*can, must, do* ...) ne sont en général pas accentués.

CLASSE CD • 2 04

c. **Lis les phrases suivantes et entoure les mots qui sont accentués selon toi. Puis écoute et vérifie.**

I'm watching an old film on television with my sister.

Where's he going tonight?

B Hurry up! ➪ Manuel, p. 67

1 • Link the actions to the times.

The plane is leaving •	• at 6.20 am.
Mr and Mrs Brown are leaving •	• in ten minutes.
The plane is landing •	• at 6.10 pm.

DID YOU KNOW?

Il y a 5 heures de décalage horaire entre New York et Londres et 6 heures entre New York et Paris. Lorsqu'il est midi à New York, il est 18 heures à Paris.

Quelle heure est-il à New York au moment où tu lis cette rubrique ? ....

Combien de temps dure le vol de Mr Brown ? ....

2 • Tick the correct answers.

a. Mrs Brown is looking for ❑ her book ❑ the keys ❑ the tickets.

b. Apparently, they ❑ are ❑ aren't in the kitchen.

c. Lily thinks ❑ Alex ❑ Justin ❑ Mr Brown took them.

3 • If someone took them, circle who.

Lily Alex Justin Mr Brown

4 • Recap.

Mr and Mrs Brown .... to the airport in ten minutes, but Mrs Brown is worried.

She can't find the ....

Conclude.

The keys were ❑ nowhere ❑ somewhere in the kitchen.

Lily isn't happy because ❑ no one listens to her ❑ someone listened to her.

Grammar bag Les composés de *some, any* et *no*

Get it.

1. Observe les phrases suivantes.

a. *Are they visiting anyone?* ......

b. *No one is sleeping!* ......

c. *Look, there's someone in the garden.* ......

d. *The book is somewhere in my bag.* ......

e. *Are you going anywhere?* ......

f. *No, I'm not going anywhere today!* ......

g. *My shoes are nowhere in my room!* ......

2. Note sur les pointillés s'il s'agit d'une phrase affirmative (A), négative (N) ou interrogative (I).

● Tu te souviens que dans *something, anything* et *nothing, -thing* fait référence à un **objet**.
Ici, quel mot fait référence à un **lieu** ? ....
Quel mot fait référence à une **personne** ? ....

● *Something, someone, somewhere* et leurs composés fonctionnent comme ***some, any*** et ***no***.
Pour parler de la présence ou l'absence de quelqu'un (« quelqu'un »/« personne »), on utilise :
– .... dans les formes interrogatives et négatives,
– .... dans les formes affirmatives (« quelqu'un »),
– .... dans les formes affirmatives (« personne »).
Pour parler d'un lieu (« quelque part »/« nulle part »), on utilise :
– .... dans les formes interrogatives et négatives,
– .... dans les formes affirmatives (« quelque part »),
– .... dans les formes affirmatives (« nulle part »).

In the bag.

Complète par le composé de *some, any* ou *no* qui convient.

a. Mum, there isn't .... in the fridge. We must go shopping.

b. "Is there .... in the bathroom?" "No, there isn't."

c. I'm sure he's in the kitchen eating .... He's always hungry!

d. He was sad because .... came to his party!

e. I know he lives .... behind the school.

f. Look, there is .... sleeping in our garden!

Take your pen.

Écris une histoire mystérieuse.

Tu es réveillé(e) en pleine nuit : tu entends du bruit dans ta chambre / ta maison et tu distingues aussi des formes. Il y a quelque chose ou quelqu'un ! Raconte la scène.

I'm in the dark, I can't .... but ....

....

....

....

Do you remember?

1 • Que mets-tu comme vêtements lorsqu'il fait froid ?

a. a s.................. b. a s............. c. a w.............. .. .. d. g..............

2 • Qu'emportes-tu avec toi lorsqu'il pleut ?

a. a .... b. an ....

3 • Retrouve les mots correspondant aux définitions.

a. Send messages on your mobile. → ....

b. Talk to a friend. → ....

c. Means of transport in the sky. → ....

4 • Rédige ce que les Jenkins ont prévu.

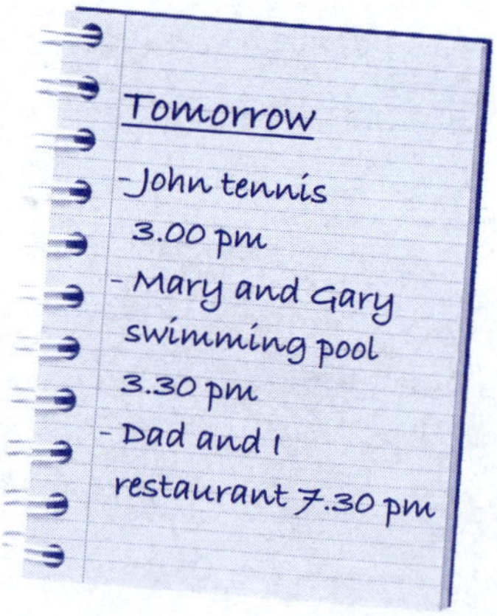

....

....

....

....

....

....

5 • Complète à l'aide des éléments proposés.

no one • something • anything • anywhere • someone • nothing

"Are you doing .... special tomorrow?"

"I'm meeting .... at 7 pm."

"Oh, and where are you going?"

"We aren't going .... We're just eating .... at home.
What about you, what are you doing?"

"Well, ...! ....'s here this weekend!"

TAKE 2 At home!

Warm up. ➪ Manuel, p. 70

Complete the labels.

.... hair →

a .... →

long .... hair →

← long .... hair

← a ....

A What a day! ➪ Manuel, p. 70

1 • Mr Brown's problems

a. Mr Brown had problems with ❑ 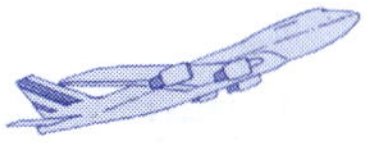 ❑ 

❑  ❑  ❑ 

b. When he arrived, Mr Brown looked for ❑  ❑ 

c. Mr Brown is ❑ surprised ❑ exhausted.

2 • At home: Listen and tick the correct answer.

a. On the table, Mr Brown found ❑  ❑ 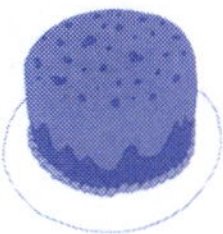

b. Mr Brown thinks ❑ Meg's really kind. ❑ Meg isn't nice at all.

c. Mr Brown saw ❑  ❑ 

3 • Recap: Complete the sentences with the correct adjective.

happy • scared • exhausted • bad

When Mr Brown arrived, he was .... so he was very .... to be back home.

But suddenly, he was a little .... because he saw someone in the garden!

Mr Brown had a .... day!

Conclude.

Complete Mr Brown's words.

What ....!

I CAN do it!

➪ Manuel, *p. 57*

› Comment apprendre mes verbes irréguliers ?

Pense à ajouter *break* dans ton jeu de cartes et profites-en pour réviser tous tes verbes !

Grammar bag — Les phrases exclamatives

Get it.

1. Observe les phrases suivantes.

a. *What an expensive car!*

b. *How strange!*

c. *What a trip!*

d. *How ridiculous!*

2. Encadre en noir les mots exclamatifs et souligne en bleu l'élément sur lequel porte l'exclamation.

● Pour faire une phrase exclamative, on peut utiliser :

– .... + adj.

Ex. : .... *nice!*

– .... + *a / an* (+ adj.) + nom au singulier.

Ex. : .... *a car!* .... *an expensive car!*

Attention !

Devant un nom au pluriel, on n'utilise pas de déterminant.

*Ex. : **What** nice shoes!*

In the bag.

Complète les phrases suivantes avec le mot exclamatif qui convient.

a. .... a great film! I loved it!

b. There's nothing on television again. .... boring!

c. Oh, Bruce! .... a nice surprise! And .... lovely flowers! Thank you!

The Music of English

Les intonations des phrases exclamatives. ➪ Manuel, *p. 70*

CLASSE CD • 2 09

a. **Écoute les phrases suivantes.**

What an expensive car! ...... *How stupid!* ...... *What big trees!* ......

b. **Note ↘ si la voix descend ou ↗ si la voix monte en fin de phrase.**

Dans les phrases exclamatives, l'intonation est toujours ....

c. **Répète à présent les phrases ci-dessus.**

B Changes ➪ Manuel, *p. 71*

1 • Lucifer and Meg changed in 6 months. Listen and circle the correct pictures.

a1 

a2 

b1 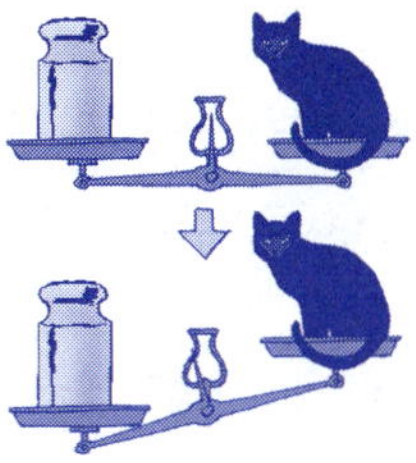

b2 

c1 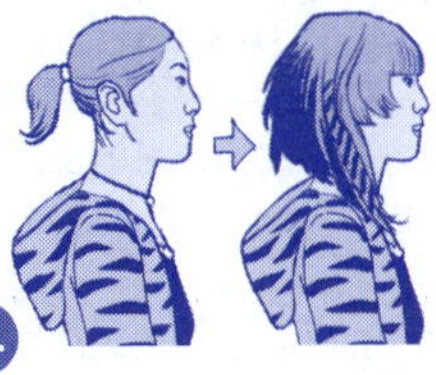

c2 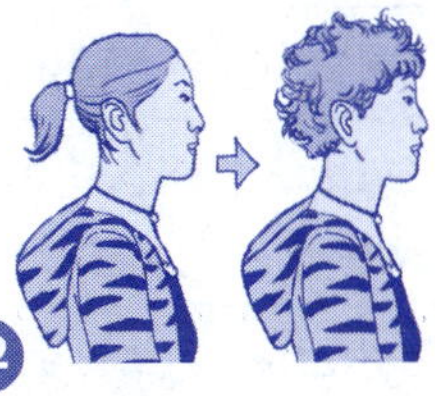

2 • Listen and link Meg or Justin to what they are now. Cross the odd one out.

Justin ●
Meg ●

● better at science
● more athletic
● better singer

3 • Recap: Complete the sentences.

Lucifer is .... and .... now.

Meg is more .... than before.

Justin has got .... marks at science.

Conclude.

Meg and Justin ❑ are ❑ aren't very good friends!

I CAN do it!

➪ Manuel, *p. 35*

> Comment apprendre mon vocabulaire ? (1)

Regroupe sous la forme d'un soleil les mots liés à la **chevelure** *(hair)*.

Grammar bag **Le comparatif de supériorité**

Get it.

1. Observe les phrases suivantes.

a. *He's taller than his brother.*

b. *Their house is bigger than my house!*

c. *The film is scarier than the book.*

d. *Mum is more athletic than Dad.*

e. *I didn't play well but John was worse than me!*

f. *Yummy, the carrots are better than the beans!*

2. Repère les adjectifs.
Souligne en bleu la terminaison commune des adjectifs dans les phrases a, b et c.
Dans la phrase d, encadre en bleu ce que l'on a ajouté devant l'adjectif.
Encadre en rouge les adjectifs au comparatif dans les phrases e et f.

3. Encadre en vert le mot qui sert à introduire le deuxième élément de la comparaison.

4. Réécris les adjectifs de base des phrases a à f.

a. .... c. .... e. ....

b. .... d. .... f. ....

Adjectifs courts adj. + -..........	1 syllabe : *tall* → *tall......* 2 syllabes si l'adjectif se termine par *-y* : *scary* → *scari......*
Adjectifs longs .... + adj.	2 syllabes si l'adjectif ne se termine pas par *-y* : *tired* → .... *tired* 3 syllabes et plus : *athletic* → .... *athletic*

● .... permet d'introduire le deuxième terme de la comparaison.

Cas particuliers :
– Lorsque l'adjectif se termine par *– y*, le *– y* se transforme en *– i*.
Ex. : *happy* → ....
– Les adjectifs d'une syllabe se terminant par une consonne précédée d'une seule voyelle doublent la consonne finale.
Ex. : *big* → ....
– Certains adjectifs sont irréguliers. Apprends-les par cœur.
Ex. : *good* → .... *bad* → ....

In the bag.

Compare les éléments à l'aide des adjectifs proposés.

a. Sandra / pretty / her sister.

....

b. The second song / good / the first song.

....

c. The blue T-shirt / expensive / the white T-shirt.

....

d. August / hot / March.

....

e. John / jealous / his sister.

....

You're the actor!

⇨ Manuel, *p. 71*

Pupil A: Imagine Oki and prepare your instructions.

1 • Complete the bag with adjectives you can use to compare Oki with Oko.

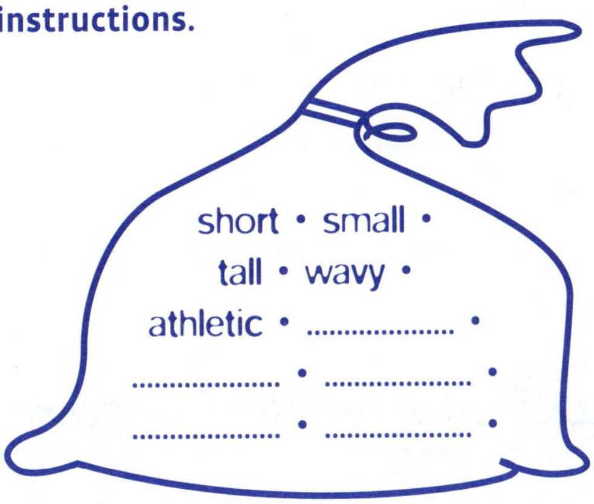

2 • Compare Oki with Oko and write your instructions on a piece of paper.

Oki is more .... than Oko, because he's got a tennis racket.

He's got .... eyes than Oko.

Oki is better at .... because he's got ....

Pupil B: Read Pupil A's instructions and draw Oki on a piece of paper.
Then show Pupil A your drawing.

Pupils A and B: Check if the drawing is correct.

Astuce

Rappelle-toi que pour comparer deux éléments :
– si l'adjectif que tu utilises est **court**, tu dois ajouter *-er* ;
Ex.: She is shorter than Oki.
– si l'adjectif est **long**, tu ajoutes more devant l'adjectif.
Ex.: Oki is more athletic than Oko.

Relis les adjectifs que tu as écrits dans le sac et entoure en bleu les adjectifs courts. Puis vérifie que tu as bien construit les comparatifs.

Do you remember?

1 • Écris de mémoire 5 adjectifs pour qualifier la chevelure.

....

2 • Quelle mot anglais décrit une coiffure en utilisant un nom d'animal ? ....

**3 • Tu as fait une surprise à ta grand-mère et elle est très contente.
Complète sa bulle de parole.**

What ....!
....!

**4 • Rédige des phrases complètes en comparant les deux éléments soulignés.
Attention : tu dois utiliser *be* ou *have got*, selon le sens de la phrase.**

a. Her cat / big / my dog!

....

b. My sister / curly hair / my brother.

....

c. Ben / good marks / me.

....

d. The book / interesting / the film.

....

e. The twins / tall / Ben.

....

TAKE 3 *Back home for the holidays*

Warm up.

➪ Manuel, *p. 74*

Write the words under the correct pictures.

freezing cold • a blizzard • snow • icy • overcast • rainy

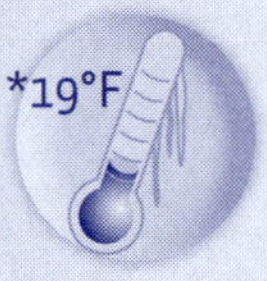

a ....

b ....

c ....

d ....

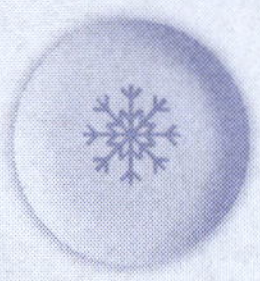

e ....

f ....

DID YOU KNOW?

Les Américains utilisent le Fahrenheit comme unité de mesure pour la température. Si tu as 37°C, qu'indiquera le thermomètre en Fahrenheit ?

.... °F

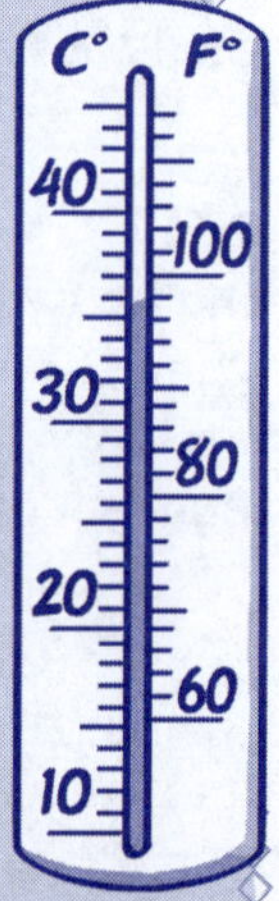

A Preparing the winter holidays ➪ Manuel, p. 74

1 • What do Justin and Mr Brown say in the conversation?

Link the correct pictures to the countries.

Great Britain ● United States of America ●

2 • Tick the correct answers.

a. Mr Brown thinks winter is ❑ the most beautiful season ❑ the most dangerous season ❑ the best season of the year.

b. In the USA, yesterday was ❑ the coldest ❑ the hottest ❑ the sunniest day of the year.

3 • Circle the correct answers.

a. At school, Justin is studying

b. *The Canterbury Tales* is a book a film an attraction a city.

c. Chaucer is ❑ a character in the book ❑ the author of the book ❑ Alex and Justin's teacher.

4 • Link the correct elements from the two columns.

Justin read the book ●	● last year.
Justin visited the attraction ●	● last month.
	● when he was young.

5 • Tick the correct answers.

a. Who's going to do the presentation to the class?

❑ Mr Brown. ❑ Justin. ❑ Justin and Alex. ❑ The teacher.

b. The teacher thinks Justin and Alex are the best because ❑ they are British ❑ they read the book last year ❑ they love *The Canterbury Tales*.

c. Justin ❑ loves this attraction ❑ loved this attraction when he was younger.

6 • Recap.

Justin is unhappy because he must make a presentation about ....

and ❑ he doesn't like his teacher ❑ he doesn't like working during the holidays

❑ he doesn't like doing presentations.

Conclude.

Justin is ❑ hard-working ❑ a bit lazy.

Grammar bag — Le superlatif

Get it.

1. Observe les phrases suivantes.

a. *It's the coldest day of the year.*

b. *I want the biggest ice cream in the shop.*

c. *Yesterday was the rainiest day of the week.*

d. *It's the most dangerous season of the year.*

e. *We're the best in the family.*

f. *It was the worst day of my life.*

2. Dans ces phrases, on compare ❑ **deux éléments entre eux**

❑ **un élément avec un ensemble d'autres éléments.**

3. Repère les adjectifs.

Souligne en bleu la terminaison commune des adjectifs dans les phrases a, b et c.

Dans la phrase d, encadre en bleu le mot que l'on a ajouté devant l'adjectif.

Encadre en rouge les adjectifs au superlatif dans les phrases e et f.

4. Dans chaque phrase, encadre en vert le mot commun qui précède l'adjectif.

5. Entoure en noir les prépositions qui suivent le superlatif.

.... fait référence à un lieu ou des personnes. .... s'utilise dans les autres cas.

6. Réécris les adjectifs de base des phrases a à f.

a. .... c. .... e. ....

b. .... d. .... f. ....

● On utilise le **superlatif** pour comparer .... élément avec .... d'autres éléments.
Comme pour le comparatif, on distingue les adjectifs **courts** et les adjectifs **longs**.

Adjectifs courts	1 syllabe : *cold* → *the cold......*
.... + adj. + -.......	2 syllabes si l'adjectif se termine par *-y* : *rainy* → *the raini......*
Adjectifs longs	2 syllabes si l'adjectif ne se termine pas par *-y* : *tired* → *the* .... *tired*
.... + adj.	3 syllabes et plus : *dangerous* → *the* .... *dangerous*

● Les prépositions .... (pour les lieux ou les personnes) ou .... (pour les autres cas) introduisent le deuxième ensemble d'éléments.

Attention !
On n'utilise plus ***than*** dans le superlatif !

Cas particuliers :
– Les **modifications orthographiques** sont les mêmes que pour le comparatif de supériorité.
⇨ Manuel, p. 76.
– Les **adjectifs irréguliers** : *good* → the .... *bad* → the ....

In the bag.

Qui est le meilleur de la classe dans sa catégorie ?

Tom	Gary	Sonia
maths: B	maths: A	maths: B –
1.45 m	1.41 m	1.46 m
lazy +++	lazy –	lazy +
athletic +	athletic ++	athletic –

a. Tom .... the class.
b. Sonia .... the class.
c. Gary .... the class.
d. Gary .... the class.

The Music of English

L'accentuation des mots en *-ic*. ⇨ Manuel, *p. 74*

CLASSE CD 2 13
a. **Écoute les mots suivants et entoure la syllabe accentuée.**
fantastic • allergic • artistic • electric • economic

Lorsqu'un mot se termine par le suffixe ...., c'est ❑ la dernière ❑ l'avant-dernière syllabe qui est accentuée.

CLASSE CD 2 14
b. **Encadre la syllabe accentuée des mots en *-ic* ci-dessous puis dis ces séries à voix haute.**
***dra**ma* → *dramatic* • ***ar**tist* → *artistic* • *e**co**nomy* → *economic* •
***his**tory* → *historic* • ***sym**bol* → *symbolic*

c. **Écoute et vérifie.**

B Visiting Canterbury

➪ Manuel, *p. 75*

1 • Read the document and say which attraction is the best for these people.

a. Mary: “I like listening to old stories.” ....

b. Greg: “I’m interested in the life of prisoners in medieval times.” ....

c. Gary: “I love very old monuments from the Middle Ages.” ....

2 • Right or wrong? Justify by quoting from the text.

a. Canterbury Cathedral is quite recent. ❑ Right. ❑ Wrong.

....

b. The West Gate is a very big old city gate. ❑ Right. ❑ Wrong.

....

c. Some people live in Canterbury Castle today. ❑ Right. ❑ Wrong.

....

d. There are more tourists at the Canterbury Tales attraction than at the cathedral.
❑ Right. ❑ Wrong.

....

Do you remember?

1 • Écris les expressions liées à la météo sous les dessins.

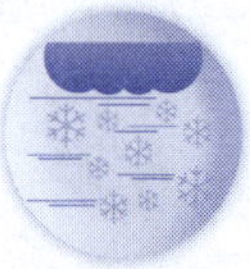

a. .... b. .... c. .... d. .... e. ....

2 • Écris les mots correspondant aux définitions.

a. fantastic → ....

b. a place where you keep prisoners → a ....

c. a city or castle entrance → a ....

3 • Complète les phrases à l’aide des adjectifs proposés au superlatif.

popular • bad • cold • good

a. February is .... month of the year.

b. Winter is .... season for driving! It’s too dangerous!

c. You have .... view of the city from the top of the tower.

d. The cathedral is very famous. It’s .... monument in the city!

CULTURE CORNER England in the Middle Ages

➪ Manuel, *pp. 78-79*

A *The Normans in England*

1. Draw William the Conqueror's route on the map.

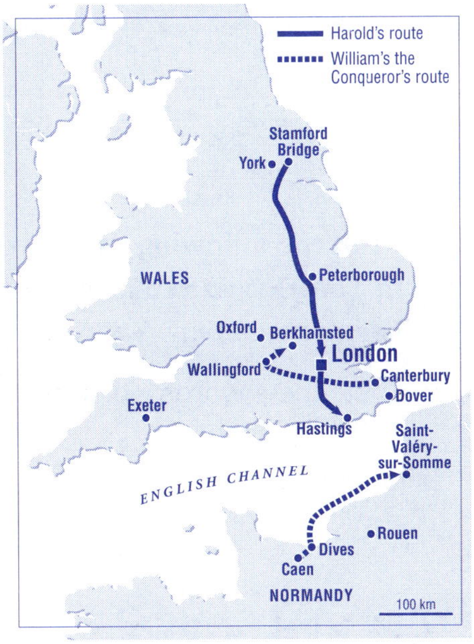

DID YOU KNOW?

La Tapisserie de Bayeux raconte l'histoire de la conquête de l'Angleterre par les Normands en 1066. Elle a été brodée entre 1066 et 1082, et fait environ 68 mètres de long sur 50 centimètres de large ! Elle a été ensuite exposée dans la Cathédrale de Bayeux, en Normandie, pour que la population française, qui ne savait pas toujours lire, puisse découvrir l'histoire de Guillaume le Conquérant (*William the Conqueror.*)

[Group A] [Group B] [Group A]

Title: ....

2. Give the scene a title.

3. Guess who the Saxons are and who the Normans are.

The Normans are ❑ group A ❑ group B.

4. Tick the correct answers.

a. William the Conqueror was ❑ French ❑ English.

b. The English ❑ lost ❑ won the Battle of Hastings in 1066.

c. William and his army stopped ❑ in Hastings ❑ in London.

B Words!

1. Correct the information by quoting from the text.

a. In the Middle Ages, the Normans spoke Saxon. ❑ Right. ❑ Wrong.

....

b. There are very few traces of French in English today. ❑ Right. ❑ Wrong.

....

2. Read the following list of words.

pork • beef • cow • calf • mutton • sheep • veal • pig

a. Circle the 4 words which come from French.

b. Complete the chart.

Cooked meat (Norman words)	Live animals (Anglo-Saxon words)
pork	pig
....	....
....	....
....	....

Did you know?
Geoffrey Chaucer and The Canterbury Tales

1. Read the sentences about Geoffrey Chaucer. Underline what's wrong and correct the information.

a. Geoffrey Chaucer died when he was 43 years old.

....

b. He wrote stories for the English King.

....

c. In *The Canterbury Tales*, a man and his wife travel to Canterbury.

....

2. Read the beginning of *The Wife of Bath's Tale* and do the activities.

a. Tick the correct answers.

❑ Tarquin loved Lucretia. ❑ Lucretia loved Tarquin. ❑ Tarquin kidnapped Lucretia.

b. Cross out the wrong sentence.

1. King Arthur wanted to help Lucretia.
2. King Arthur's knights found where Tarquin was.
3. King Arthur thought kidnapping a woman wasn't a serious crime.

3. In the second part of *The Wife of Bath*, Queen Guinevere, King Arthur's wife, saves Tarquin's life because he understood a very important thing.
Complete with the missing vowels to discover what Tarquin understood.

O • E • E • E • E • U

M _ N M _ ST R _ SP _ CT W _ M _ N

The Spotlight

Out in Greenwich

➪ Manuel, p. 80

Do you remember the video?

Write captions or fill in the balloons.

PART 1

Greenwich, London.

PART 2

In front of Trafalgar Tavern.

DID YOU KNOW?

Horatio Nelson (1758-1805) was an officer in the Royal Navy. He became very famous with his victory over the French and Spanish navy at the Battle of Trafalgar in 1805. That's why there is a statue of Nelson in the middle of Trafalgar Square in London.

PROJECT *My travel blog!* ➪ Manuel, *p. 81*

1. Go to the indicated site and do the activities.
http://www.welcome-hatier.com

a. Find the name of the official residence of the Queen.

....

b. You ❑ can ❑ can't visit Tower Bridge.

c. Find on the site the name of a famous cathedral.

....

d. The Houses of Parliament have more rooms than Buckingham Palace.

❑ True. ❑ False.

e. What is the name of the big clock in London?

....

f. The National Gallery is a museum ❑ for adults only ❑ for adults and children.

g. The London Dungeon is ❑ a scary place ❑ a romantic place.

g. What can you see from the London Eye?

.... / ....

2. Get ready to write your blog. Imagine ...

a. what time you're leaving: ....

b. what means of transport you're taking: ....

c. your lunch (place/type): . ...

d. Choose two monuments you're visiting tomorrow with your family.

Monument 1	**Monument 2**
Adjectives to describe it:	Adjectives to describe it: ....
Information about this monument:	Information about this monument: ....

CHECK YOUR PROGRESS ☹ 😐 ☺

MON GUIDE D'AUTO-ÉVALUATION

➩ Manuel, p. 82

Vocabulary challenge

Can you find the nineteen words of the workshop?

Tu as trouvé • moins de 7 mots ☹ • de 8 à 15 mots 😐 • plus de 16 mots ☺.

Down

1. It protects your clothes from the rain.
2. When it's very cold, the roads are ...
3. It protects your neck from the cold.
4. A part of your hair.
5. A storm with snow.
6. Send messages from a mobile.
7. They protect your hands from the cold.
8. When you take a test, you can have a good or a bad ...
9. Opposite of "light".
10. Where you keep a prisoner.

Across

3. Opposite of "curly".
7. Entrance to a city or a castle.
11. You stand under it when it's raining.
12. A way of doing your hair.
13. Very tired.
14. Impolite.
15. Between straight and curly.
16. Means of transport in the sky.
17. Hair with spikes.

1. Check your vocabulary.

Tu as trouvé • moins de 6 mots ☹ • de 7 à 10 mots 😐 • plus de 10 mots ☺.

2. Check your tools.

a. What are they doing now? What are they doing this afternoon?

Tu as conjugué correctement des verbes au *be* + BV-*ing*.

• Jamais. ☹ • Parfois. 😐 • Toujours. ☺

Tu as utilisé des composés de *some*. • Oui. ☺ • Non. ☹

b. Imagine your parents want to buy one of these three dogs. Which one do you prefer? Compare them.

Tes comparatifs de supériorité étaient corrects.

• Jamais. ☹ • Parfois. 😐 • Toujours. ☺

Tes superlatifs étaient corrects.

• Jamais. ☹ • Parfois. 😐 • Toujours. ☺

c. Your best friend arrives with one of these dogs. Imagine your reactions.

Tes phrases exclamatives étaient correctes.

• Jamais. ☹ • Parfois. 😐 • Toujours. ☺

Quand tu as entouré ☹ ou 😐, révise le point concerné :

2. a. ⇨ Manuel, *p. 68* : Le présent en *be* + BV-*ing*.

2. b. ⇨ Manuel, *p. 72* : Comparer.
⇨ Manuel, *p. 76* : Le superlatif.

2. c. ⇨ Manuel, *p. 68* : S'exclamer.

A DOG IN THE CITY

➪ Manuel, p. 37

1. Watch Part 1 of the video without the sound.

a. Where's Pip, the dog? ....

b. Imagine his feelings and tick the correct answers.

❑ happy ❑ angry ❑ sad ❑ hungry ❑ tired

c. Circle the two things the young woman and Pip have in common.

They need help. • They're rich. • People don't look at them.

d. Imagine what the young man is going to do.

....

2. Watch the video.

a. Listen to the music and circle the correct sentence.

First, the music is happy, then it's sad.

First, the music is sad, then it's happy.

b. Why does the music change?

....

c. Tick the correct answer.

❑ The RSPCA is a zoo.

❑ The RSPCA is a music school.

❑ The RSPCA helps animals without a home.

THE GOLD RUSH

➪ Manuel, p. 59

1. Watch the scene and tick the correct answer.

a. The scene takes place in a ❑ poor cabin ❑ rich house.

b. The two characters are ❑ very poor ❑ very rich.

DID YOU KNOW?

Charlie Chaplin's parents were poor music hall artists. When he was a child, Chaplin was often hungry and he never forgot poor people in his films.

c. Whose boot is it? ❑ The Tramp's. ❑ The other character's.

d. The boot is ❑ hot ❑ cold.

e. Why does the man change plates? ❑ He doesn't want to eat.
❑ He wants a lot of "food".

f. Who starts eating? ❑ The Tramp. ❑ The other character.

g. The Tramp is ❑ happy ❑ sad ❑ disappointed.

h. At the end, the two characters ❑ are ❑ aren't eating the boot.

2. Watch the scene again and imagine the dialogue between the two characters.

....

....

....

....

....

....

....

....

CULTURE CORNER Scotland's many faces

(SUPPORT D'ACTIVITÉ)

➪ Manuel, p. 26

A Discover Scottish traditions

2. A Scottish legend

Send your teacher a postcard from Loch Ness.
Cut it out and colour it in. Then complete your message on the back of the postcard.

Dear teacher,

I'm at Loch Ness. Nessie is in front of me!

She's got ....

....

....

....

....

....

....

....

....

....

....

□□□□□□ ....

I CAN do it !

➪ Manuel, p. 57

Quel est le prétérit de *lose* ?	Quelle est la base verbale de *bought* ?	GIVE → GAVE	TAKE → TOOK
Quel est le prétérit de *run* ?	Quelle est la base verbale de *taught* ?	RIDE → RODE	BUY → BOUGHT
Quel est le prétérit de *go* ?	Quelle est la base verbale de *thought* ?	EAT → ATE	LEAVE → LEFT

WENT	THINK	MANGER	PARTIR
RAN	TEACH	FAIRE DU CHEVAL / VÉLO	ACHETER
LOST	BUY	DONNER	PRENDRE